GUARDING THE MOUNTAIN MAN'S SECRET

BROTHERS OF SAPPHIRE RANCH
BOOK SEVEN

MISTY M. BELLER

Misty M. Beller
BOOKS

ISBN-13 Trade Paperback: 978-1-965918-00-5

ISBN-13 Large Print Paperback: 978-1-965918-02-9

ISBN-13 Casebound Hardback: 978-1-965918-03-6

Where can I go from Your Spirit?
Or where can I flee from Your presence?

If I ascend into heaven, You are there;
If I make my bed in hell, behold, You are there.

If I take the wings of the morning,
And dwell in the uttermost parts of the sea,

Even there Your hand shall lead me,
And Your right hand shall hold me.

Psalm 139:7-10 (NKJV)

CHAPTER 1

*D*ecember, 1870
Rock Creek, Montana Territory

The late-afternoon sky stretched in a canvas of rich blue as Clara Pendleton guided her horse along the trail. What a blessing to be on this journey rather than living in luxury back East with a man she'd never loved—a man she'd feared. Papa had approved her breaking the engagement and leaving town, but would he pay for their decision?

All she could do was pray and put him in God's care.

The surveyor's mount ambled in front of her, Mr. Goodwin's lanky body swaying with each step. Ahead of him rode grumpy Mr. Tillman and Mr. Holloway, hired by the railroad to lead this motley surveying crew.

She glanced back at Uncle Hiram, who met her look with that warm smile that deepened the creases around his eyes. He rode these mountains like he'd grown up in them, not on his Virginia farm. He'd been the one to put her on her first horse, though, when she'd gone to stay with him as a young girl while Papa took Mama to one of her many expensive medical treatments. Uncle Hiram's farm had been like heaven to her girlish cravings for adventure. All her life, Uncle Hiram had been the steady presence that settled her.

Behind him rode the final member of their group, Mr. Whitaker. He always took up the rear when they traveled, probably to spot every movement each of them made. The man wore suspicion like a pair of trousers.

The land around them tilted upward as they ascended a hillside covered in pine trees and rocks that crunched under their horses' hooves. The ground here wasn't nearly as rugged as some places they'd ridden this past week. In those spots, she'd needed to focus all her attention on staying seated while her horse navigated rocks and steep slopes. But up ahead, the trail leveled out again, and she'd be able to enjoy the view without worrying about tumbling off her mount.

Even now, she could see mountain peaks through the trees, rising to the west with snow-capped peaks. Such majesty. What would it be like to live here year round?

Her fingers tingled, itching to pull out her sketch pad and draw this terrain. But first things first. Once they reached the top of the rise, she'd mark these details on the map she kept rolled up in her saddle bag.

Every day since she'd left home to meet up with Uncle Hiram and the rest of these men, she'd thanked God for giving her the courage to not marry Nathaniel MacGregor. Even if her decision meant Papa lost his job at the factory owned by Nathaniel's father.

Surely the man wouldn't punish her father for something *she'd* done. At least that was what Papa had assured her—over and over again after she'd called off the wedding.

Papa couldn't afford to lose his position as foreman at MacGregor's Upholstery. As hard as he worked and as much as she and her stepmother had tried to cut costs, they had no savings. One injury, one lost paycheck, would leave her father and Sarah with scarcely enough to survive the week.

He'd said that was his concern, not hers. That she should come work with Uncle Hiram if she wanted. She'd taken him at his word, and even though she still worried, she'd not once regretted coming here. Spending time with her uncle, seeing new country every day—she loved it all. Even living out of her carpet bag for weeks on end wasn't so bad. It certainly beat becoming Mrs. MacGregor.

At the front of the line, Mr. Holloway straightened in his saddle, raising his hand for a halt. "Do you hear that?"

Along with the others, she reined in her mare, then strained to listen. A pounding noise. Like rock against rock. Or maybe against metal. A steady rhythm.

She scanned the mountainside ahead of them. They'd not seen anyone since leaving their camp beside the main road that morning.

Mr. Goodwin shaded his eyes with his hand. "Yessir. You think someone's mining this far away from the creek?"

Mr. Holloway's mouth formed a grim line. "Keep your guns ready."

She touched the pistol tucked into her waistband. She wouldn't shoot a man, but Holloway and even Uncle Hiram had insisted she carry the weapon. Just in case she met with a wild animal, though Holloway had said such a small charge would only anger a grizzly. That if she met with a bear, she should aim at the sky to call for help. Surely a gunshot would be more than an irritant, though, even to the fierce bears that were said to inhabit this land.

Mr. Holloway started his mount walking again, and she nudged Rosie forward when their turn came.

The pounding grew louder as they rode up the sloping trail.

Then it ceased, and Holloway's hand shot up for them to halt once more.

"Who are you?" A man's voice sounded ahead, much closer

than expected, and she rose up in her saddle to see over those riding in front of her.

A stranger stood in the trail ahead, beside a rocky cliff. Because of her obstructed view, she only saw the man's head—a shock of brown hair and a handsome face, though younger than she'd expected. She spied intelligence in his eyes even from this distance.

Mr. Holloway's voice was strong. "We're a surveying crew, sent by the railroad. Do you own this property?"

"My family does." The stranger eyed them warily as he shifted. The movement brought a bit more of him into view, including the rifle held loosely in his muscular arms. "What business does the railroad have here?"

Mr. Holloway kept his tone even. "We've been commissioned to survey the area around the Mullan Road, to assess its suitability for a new rail line. If the railroad wants to proceed, they'll contact the owners later."

A scowl twisted his handsome features, crinkling lines between his brows. "This land isn't for sale."

Mr. Holloway gave a slight smile, pulling out the manners he used only in these situations. "I understand, and you can say as much then. Our job is only to survey and map the terrain." He glanced up and down the slope. "Any place you recommend for a good spot to camp? We'll only be here a couple nights, then we'll move on."

The stranger tipped his head to the side. Was he thinking of running them off the land? That hadn't happened to them yet, though she'd worried a few homesteaders would attempt to. Finally, he pointed west toward the creek at the bottom of the slope they'd just climbed. "Back down there's a level bit on the other side of the creek, not far from water. It'll serve well enough for a camp."

Mr. Holloway dipped his chin. "Much obliged. We'll be on our way, then."

As the group turned their horses downhill, she couldn't resist another glance at the stranger. This time, he met her gaze directly, curiosity flickering in his warm eyes. She offered him a friendly smile, something she would do for anyone she met.

After a moment's hesitation, the corners of his mouth lifted, and he gave a polite nod.

A niggle of pleasure wove through her. She doubted she'd ever see this man again.

Who was he? He appeared a little older than her eighteen years, but the way he stood with that rifle in hand made him look like he belonged in this mountain wilderness. As though he knew every crack and crevice and could scale them if he chose.

Had he grown up here? What was his story?

She likely wouldn't get a chance to learn any of those answers, so she shifted her focus back to navigating the rocky terrain. She had work to do, people counting on her. She couldn't be distracted by a handsome face.

~

*H*ow could he be so careless? As soon as the group moved on, Miles Coulter eased out a breath.

Strangers on the ranch.

And they nearly caught him unaware.

He'd been testing out the latest version of the jointed pickax he'd designed—a modification of one he'd seen in Canvas City—when he barely caught the sounds of horse hooves on rock. He managed to drop the tool and scoop up his rifle in time to face them as they rode around the bend in the trail.

Surveyors. From the railroad. What would his brother Jericho say about that? He'd not like it.

At least they weren't Mick's men, come to exact revenge on their brother Gil. Thank the Lord, Mick's daughter escaped the man's evil clutches with their help, but they still watched out for any sign of his thugs.

Even if Miles suspected these surveyors were presenting a ruse, the woman with them couldn't be one of Mick's guards.

He pictured the woman's pretty young face. She'd been a surprise, for certain. She wore a fancy bonnet like the ladies in town did, and a dark blue dress that looked soft and shiny. An unusual sight in a group of men like that. Too fancy to be their cook.

She must be married to one of them. A surveyor's wife willing to brave the wild frontier to be with her man.

Usually, a thought like that would make him chuckle. Or even scoff. But a fellow lucky enough to have a lady like her... well, he should count his blessings.

Speaking of which, where had he dropped his ax? There, half buried in the dirt. He reached for the tool and swung it over his shoulder, then started for the house. He'd need to tell the others right away.

When Miles entered the yard, Gil stood in front of the barn, saddling one of the two-year-old geldings. "How'd your invention work? See anything unusual out there?"

How long would it take for his brother to stop looking over his shoulder for Mick's men? It had been weeks already since Gil and Jude brought Jess home with them, with the help of Two Stones. Of course, Gil had taken quite a beating in the process. Broken ribs took months to fully heal. But he probably lingered close to the house now so he'd be ready to protect Jess should her father's guards come after them.

Miles leaned the pickax against the barn wall. "Met riders."

Gil straightened. "Who?" Worry filled his gaze, though concern rarely left his expression these days. He reached for his rifle.

"Not them," Miles said, answering the question he hadn't

asked. "Surveyors, they said. For the railroad. I don't think they have anything to do with Mick."

"How could you know?" The words were a challenge, barked with anger that Miles chose to ignore. "That man is devious."

"They had a lady with them." The image of her slid into his mind, and he caught himself just before saying how pretty she was. That detail had nothing to do with whether the men were surveyors or Mick's henchmen, and in his state, Gil didn't have the patience for frivolity.

"How many were there? Where are they now?"

"Five men and the lady." Miles kept his tone steady, though Gil questioned him like he didn't know to point the strangers away from the house. "I sent them across the creek to camp. Figured Jericho would feel better with them farther away from the house and the strawberries." No one needed to find the *strawberries*—their family code word for the sapphires they mined and did their best to keep secret. Mick had found out about them, though, and his lackies stole nearly a wagon full.

If only his brothers had been willing to let that go and move on. Sampson would still be here. His brother and best friend was gone, left in the night to join Mick's underground mining crew.

The idea burned in Miles's gut.

Sampson wouldn't have joined the enemy. Not ever. His brother must be trying to make things right on his own. Sampson had already said he thought Mick's men found out about the sapphires by following him back to the ranch after a trip to town.

If only Sampson would have let the rest of them help. No single man could overcome the web of evil Mick McPharland had constructed.

Gil's frown deepened. "I don't like strangers on our land, even if they are who they claim to be."

It wasn't as if Miles had invited them. He bit back his frustration. "You sound like Jericho."

The frown turned to a glare. "You've never met Jess's father. He's more cunning than the snake in the Garden of Eden. We can't be too careful. Just because a woman is with them doesn't make them safe. Think of how they treated Jess, Mick's own daughter."

Miles sighed. "I know. But it didn't seem right to turn them away when night's coming on soon. Especially with a woman in their group."

As answer, Gil brought two fingers to his mouth and released a shrill whistle that echoed through the clearing.

Jericho and their nephew, Sean, were down the mountain helping Jonah build his new cabin. They'd be listening though. All of them were on edge these days.

Dinah, Patsy, Jess, and Lillian spilled out of the house, coming to hear what brought on the whistle. Jericho's wife—a talented doctor—Dinah would want to make sure things were ready for whatever they faced.

Patsy was Jonah's intended, and Jess would likely soon be Gil's. And Lillian... He couldn't call her his favorite niece anymore, not since two more youngsters had joined the extended family here on the ranch. But even though at thirteen she looked more young lady than girl, she still laughed at his jokes and warmed something special inside him when she called him *Uncle Miles*.

Before he and Gil could update the womenfolk, the sound of hoofbeats thundered. A minute later, Jericho, Jonah, and Sean rode up the slope from the direction of Jonah's cabin.

Another figure appeared on the trailhead leading to Eric and Naomi's cabin, moving slower on foot. Eric—Dinah's brother-in-law and an honorary member of the family. Looked like all the men were here except Jude.

He was likely on his way.

"What's going on?" Jericho reined in his horse, his sharp gaze moving between Gil and Miles.

As Miles repeated what he'd told Gil, Jericho's jaw tightened.

"And you just let them ride off to camp on our land?" Jericho shook his head. His oldest brother's fear got the better of his good sense at times.

Miles stiffened. "What would you have me do with them? Run off five men and a woman at gunpoint? Or bring them to the house so you could interrogate them?"

Jericho huffed. "What railroad do they work for? Where did they start surveying and what path are they taking? When you ask for details, you get a better idea of whether they're making up the story or not."

Miles fought the urge to roll his eyes. "Then maybe *you* better go ask those questions."

Jericho gave a curt nod. "Who's going with me? We'll have a word with our uninvited guests."

Miles's middle tightened, but he strode through the barn door, calling over his shoulder, "Let me saddle a horse. I'm coming." Jericho could ask what he wanted to the men in the group, but Miles might need to make sure he treated the lady with respect.

Jonah and Jude volunteered to come also. Good.

His eldest brother would never intentionally offend someone who didn't deserve it, but Jericho tended to be a bit overzealous when protecting his family. Especially when the threat of Mick's retaliation loomed over them all.

CHAPTER 2

a s Miles rode out with his brothers, he couldn't stop his thoughts from drifting to the woman in the surveying group. Who was she? What was her story? He needed to focus on the task at hand, but he couldn't shake the image of her luminous eyes from his mind.

He had to, though. She had to be married.

But to whom? He'd not spent much time studying the men in the group, other than the fellow in front. He had to be fifty, at least, and grizzled from plenty of time in the sun—as a surveyor would be.

The others had also looked far too old for a lady like her, hadn't they? Maybe *one* of them could be within fifteen years of her age. That taller man who rode just in front of her could be in the range.

Once more, his middle tensed. So maybe she *was* married. Not that it should bother him, but with all the pairing-up his brothers had done in the past couple of years, he couldn't help his mind going there.

The ranch had more than enough womenfolk. His brother's wives and intendeds. Not that he was looking to take a spouse anytime soon. He'd just turned eighteen last spring. He had plenty of life to live and time to find the person God had in mind. *If* God had a wife in mind for him.

On the far side of the creek, he could barely make out figures moving in the flat spot he'd told them about. When they approached, his gaze landed on the woman, kneeling beside the fire. She stood out from the other drab brown forms.

She cut vegetables into the large pot that hung over the flames, glancing up as they approached, her expression guarded.

Jericho rode straight to the man who appeared to be in charge, the older fellow with the grizzled beard who'd led their group on the trail. "I'm Jericho Coulter," he said without preamble. "This is Coulter land you're on."

As Jericho spoke with the man, who introduced himself as Emmett Holloway, Miles scanned the area. A couple of men worked at setting up tents, one tied a packhorse to a tree near the grass, and the oldest fellow in the group carried a load of wood toward the fire.

Miles's gaze kept slipping back to the woman. Every now and then, she'd look up from her task, her eyes studying him and his brothers. Each time they landed on him, his mouth found the makings of a grin.

And each time, she returned it before turning back to her work.

Now, she laid her knife aside and took up leather pads to grip the handles of the pot that sat in the blaze. Was she going to try to move that thing herself? It had to be heavy, full of water and cuttings.

Sure enough, she rose and wobbled a bit under the load. Before he could react, the older man stepped forward, motioning for her to back away as he took the pads and reached for the pot himself. She smiled at him, the affection in her eyes unmistakable. Her father, perhaps? Maybe she'd joined this group because of him, not a husband.

11

The idea gave him way too much pleasure.

Suddenly, the fellow stumbled, the weight of the pot throwing him off balance. He shuffled for his footing, finally righting himself by lowering the pot to the ground.

Water sloshed over the side and onto his gnarled hand.

His agonized scream pierced the air as he lost his grip, the pot crashing to the ground.

The woman sprang to his side. "Uncle Hiram!"

Miles leapt from his horse and sprinted, his brothers close behind. He crouched beside the fellow. "How bad is it?"

The man cradled his hand with his other and folded into himself in silent agony.

The lady gripped his shoulder. "Can I see it?"

Her uncle straightened enough for daylight to fall on the fire-red flesh. Blisters were already forming on the angry wrinkled skin.

She gasped, reaching for his cuff. "The fabric is still hot."

As she unfastened the clasp and rolled the sleeve, Miles scanned the campsite for something that might help the burn. But of course, there was nothing. "Do you have water?" Too bad they didn't have snow to numb the pain.

"Here." Another man scooped up a bucket and brought it to them. Creek water, but it looked clean enough.

The woman eased her uncle's damaged hand into the liquid, and he seemed to be fighting a cry of pain as his injury submerged.

Miles's gut twisted. That kind of pain would slay some men.

He looked around for Jericho and met his oldest brother's eyes. "We have to take him to the house."

Jericho gave a sharp nod, then turned to Holloway. "Can you saddle a horse for him? My wife's a doctor. He'll need medicine or that burn will fester. He could lose the hand."

"I'm going with him." The woman spoke up, though she kept her frowning focus on her uncle's injury.

"I will too," said Holloway.

As Miles helped the old man to his feet, his niece assisting on the other side, he caught her gaze. Up close, her eyes were a striking green, glimmering with worry. "My sister-in-law is the best doctor in the territory."

She pulled her bottom lip in. "I hope so."

Her desperation hung thick in the air. Was this uncle her last bit of family? Maybe, once Dinah had him in her care, Miles could learn more about how this intriguing lady ended up in the wilderness.

~

Clara positioned herself as near as she dared to Uncle Hiram's chair at the massive dining table in the log cabin, careful not to get in the doctor's way.

A female doctor.

Rare, indeed, and especially in this wild territory.

One of the specialists her father had taken Mama to near the end had been a female. She was said to have performed studies about unusual cures for consumption. None of her efforts with Mama had worked.

Would this lady doctor do better with her uncle's injury? Surely a burn wasn't nearly as dangerous as the awful lung disease that had wasted her mother until she had no strength left to draw breath.

Clara had heard stories of how a small wound on this dirty frontier could take a limb or even a life. And Jericho, the older, formidable man with the brooding, suspicious eyes, had suggested Uncle could lose his hand.

It could be even worse. Without proper salves and bandages, a simple cut could fester and eventually poison a person's blood. A simple injury could kill a man.

She couldn't let herself think about Uncle Hiram dying. She

loved him so much. And if he did pass, she'd be alone, miles away from civilization with nobody but a band of surveyors to protect her.

If this woman was any kind of doctor, surely she'd know how to treat a simple burn. She had to. Clara willed her breathing to slow. Once Uncle was treated, she could take over his care back at camp. She would do everything possible to heal her dear uncle.

There was a crowd in this main room of the Coulter cabin. The man they'd first met on the trail stood nearby, waiting to help as needed. He'd introduced himself as Miles Coulter, and he appeared to be the doctor's assistant or something, fetching whatever she required.

Did he normally assist? Or did he feel beholden to them because he'd been the one to meet their party first?

Jericho's glares and the questions he'd spit at Holloway proved he suspected the group of surveyors, though of what, she had no idea.

Did Miles feel the same way?

A red-haired woman and a blond girl worked by the cook-stove, and several men and a third dark-haired woman stood near the fire crackling in the hearth. Their presence didn't feel intimidating. Something about this place felt...peaceful. Rustic for sure, but between the rich aromas, the warmth of the fire, and the kindness of the people bustling around, it felt like a haven from the biting weather and the endless dirt and discomfort that came from living outdoors.

Even Dr. Coulter possessed a quiet confidence as she worked, which eased a bit of tension in Clara's chest. Would she be competent enough? Maybe Uncle Hiram's hand and arm would heal quickly. *Lord, help the injury heal quickly.*

What if it didn't? What if he lost his job with the surveyors? She would also lose hers, for she couldn't cook and draw maps for a group of men without a chaperone. Holloway would just as soon hire a man to replace her than have Uncle Hiram tag along without a purpose. The two of them would be stranded in this vast wilderness with no food or shelter.

Dr. Coulter's voice cut through her spiraling thoughts. "Keep your hand as clean as possible." She tied off the bandage she'd wrapped over the salve-soaked cloths on the burn. "The dressing should be changed twice a day at first, so I want you to come back tomorrow morning and evening. If we keep infection at bay, your recovery will go much faster."

Her uncle nodded.

Perhaps they should return to Fort Benton, the largest town she'd encountered out West thus far. Surely, a doctor there would be more competent than a housewife secluded in the mountains, one who didn't even have a clinic. Clara could find work while her uncle healed, couldn't she?

Maybe once Uncle Hiram healed, the two of them could leave surveying and mapmaking behind. They could travel farther west to California, find a quiet town to settle in. She could find work as a governess while Uncle Hiram enjoyed a slower pace. A simple existence...together, they could be content.

What other choice did she have? She'd never go back to Baltimore where Nathaniel MacGregor lived.

Holloway cleared his throat. "Mrs. Coulter, I was hoping Hiram and his niece could stay here a few nights. Until the burn starts to heal. Do you have a room available?"

Clara jerked her gaze to him. Why would he ask that? This was a home, not a clinic. And didn't he need her to cook for the crew?

Yet the lady nodded. "That's Dr. Coulter, and of course. We have room for them both."

Tightness coiled inside her. As much as she'd love to stay here in an actual house and have a doctor care for her uncle, why would Holloway send them away when *she* at least could still do her work?

As though he could hear her thoughts, Holloway locked eyes with her, his usually stern expression softening. "We'll survey the area while Hiram heals, then you two can rejoin us, and we'll all move on as before."

Was he was being kind? Or getting rid of them already?

It seemed suspicious, coming from the man who kept everyone working well past dark each night, ensuring every last task was completed. But he didn't seem to be giving her a choice.

"I can still cook," she insisted. "I can bring meals to the camp every day." Surely, she could manage that much.

Holloway nodded. "Fine." He turned to the door. "I'd best get back."

As he stepped outside, Clara inhaled a long breath and released it, forcing out as much tension with the air as possible. For now, she and her uncle were safe under the Coulters' roof— secure enough for a brief respite. Then she'd have to take on whatever challenges lay ahead on their journey.

CHAPTER 3

*C*lara tensed as she stepped ahead of Uncle Hiram from the little bed chamber Dr. Coulter had assigned them into the cabin's main room. She and her uncle had gotten settled, and now they'd been summoned for the evening meal. She was about to face a host of strangers.

The large Coulter family bustled about, a flurry of activity centered around the long, rustic dining table. The scent of roasted meat and fresh bread that filled the air had Clara's stomach growling.

She smoothed her skirts. How long had it been since she'd eaten with such a large group? Weeks at least. Since before she'd started her journey up the Missouri River on *The Loraline*.

This gathering felt far more comfortable than the meals on the steamboat had, where she'd encountered pleasant smiles and a quick kind word passed between men and women.

Miles drew out a chair, then pointed to the seat beside it. "Miss Pendleton, the two of you can sit in these."

She slid into the seat he'd pulled, and allowed him to slide her in. What an unexpected courtesy out in this frontier. Who had taught Miles such good manners?

Despite the pain he surely felt in his hand, Uncle Hiram settled in beside her and scanned the table with an excited light in his eyes. "Ladies, this meal looks magnificent. We can't thank you enough."

A smile touched Dr. Coulter's face as she waved off the compliment. "It's our pleasure. We're glad we can help."

Jericho, seated at the head beside his wife, cleared his throat, and the chatter died down. "Miles, will you ask the blessing?"

They were a Christian family then? What a relief. That explained the kindness she'd felt since arriving at the cabin—though it made her wonder anew about the eldest brother's hostility at the surveying camp.

She bowed her head with the others as Miles's rich voice sounded beside her. "Lord, thank you for this good meal and for our guests. Heal the burn quickly, Lord, and take away the pain. Please bless the food for our strength and Your service. We ask these requests in the Savior's name. Amen."

As the chorus of "Amen" echoed around the table, she opened her eyes and peeked at the man beside her. The prayer had been part frank conversation and part reverent respect. Definitely not something he'd memorized as a child and recited before each meal. And why did a younger brother pray? Where she'd come from, the eldest assumed the honor. They must take turns here.

Uncle Hiram passed a bowl of corn with his good hand, and Clara scooped a spoonful onto each of their plates. So much bounty. Vegetables and roasted meat swimming in gravy. Fresh-made biscuits. Every bite was a far cry from the limited fare she'd been able to cook over the campfire these past weeks. More than they'd usually had at home too, though her step-mother often served finer meals than they could afford on Papa's income. Even for just the three of them.

As she savored her first bite of tender roast, one of the women—Patience maybe?—turned to her with a smile. "So,

Miss Pendleton. A female in a surveying party. Do you mind if I ask how you came to join them? You must be an excellent cartographer."

Clara swallowed the bite of roast and tried to ignore the many eyes now focused on her. "Not really. I just like to draw. I guess my skill is passable enough that when Uncle Hiram mentioned me to the men in charge, they agreed to let me join."

"You're from the States then?" Patience looked truly interested, not like a gossip nosing into their affairs.

She nodded. "From Baltimore."

One of the brothers—Jonah? ...Joel? That didn't sound right. Anyway, one of the brothers spoke to Uncle Hiram. "Are you from Baltimore too, sir?"

He shook his head. "A couple hours' ride outside the city. Had me a little farm there, but I sold it when I decided I'd like to see more o' the country. Surveyin' lets me do that."

"I imagine you've seen a lot of our territory so far. Where'd you start out?" This from the oldest brother, Jericho.

"I started with the rest of the men at Fargo, and Clara joined us at Fort Benton." Uncle Hiram sent her one of those gazes so rich in love. "It sure felt like Christmas seeing her walk off that steamboat."

Christmas. That holiday would be here in a couple weeks. Maybe she could shift the conversation by asking how the Coulters celebrated the day.

Dr. Coulter spoke before she could find the words. "What made you want to leave Baltimore, Miss Pendleton? Do you have family there still?"

Did she have to tell the full truth? Maybe a part of her story would suffice. "My father and stepmother live there. I needed a change, I suppose. A fresh start. When Uncle Hiram invited me to join him, it seemed like the perfect opportunity."

She couldn't stop her gaze from sliding over to Miles, maybe because she could feel the weight of his focus. When their eyes met, his mouth curved in that small smile he often gave. But something seemed lacking in the expression this time. Had she spoken wrong?

Patience leaned forward with a sympathetic smile. "Well, we're glad to have you here. Both of you. Life in these parts can be challenging, but it's a wonderful land." She smiled lovingly at the brother Clara couldn't remember the name of. "Good people here too. The very best people."

The boy sitting on the other side of Miles—Shane? Sean?—coughed loudly enough to show how he felt about the affection dripping in Patience's voice.

The older girl beside him gave him a hard jab with her elbow, then turned to Clara with a bright smile. "You'll love it here on the ranch. You can see the mountains all around us, and the cabins stay warm in the winter. It's so pretty to look out the window and watch the snowflakes fall when you're snuggled up in a warm blanket by the fire. Do you think it'll snow soon, Uncle Jericho?" She turned that last question to the man at the head of the table.

He wiped his mouth with a serviette and shrugged. "Prob'ly so. You never know around here, but the weather's turning cold enough."

Finally, the conversation shifted away from her and Uncle Hiram, so she could relax enough to enjoy the wonderful food on her plate. The family took turns sharing funny stories or interesting tidbits from their day, sometimes ribbing each other. She'd never seen so much obvious fondness for one another, despite the occasional bickering.

It felt so different from the stiff, formal dinners at home in Baltimore, with Papa and Sarah. Conversation had been so stilted compared to this, though she'd never thought of it that way before. The questions asked and answers given among Papa, her stepmother, and herself had been superficial, as though they were only spoken from politeness. Had it been like that before Papa remarried? She couldn't remember. Those had been such dark days for them both.

Her gaze drifted to Miles, who had remained mostly quiet through the meal. He ate with a single-minded focus, as though storing up energy for some great task ahead. Yet, every so often, his eyes would flick to her, like he was attuned to her presence, her reactions.

How strange it was to be so aware of Miles. They hardly knew each other, and yet, from the moment he'd helped her from her horse, she'd felt a connection. A shared understanding, maybe, of what it was to be an outsider looking in.

She turned her attention back to her plate. It wouldn't do to let her mind wander down such paths. She was here to assist her uncle, nothing more. Once his hand healed, they would rejoin the surveying expedition, and the Coulters would fade into memory.

Still, as the evening wore on and the family began to disperse to their various pursuits, she couldn't help a pang of longing. For the warmth of the fire, the laughter ringing in the air, the sense of belonging that seemed to permeate every inch of the cabin.

This was a dangerous feeling, one she knew better than to indulge. Because she didn't belong here. Just as she hadn't belonged at home with Papa and Sarah. And especially with that rake Nathaniel MacGregor.

But as she bid the family goodnight and retreated to the small bedchamber with her uncle, she couldn't quite shake the notion that, in some strange way, she had found home.

~

lara blinked open her eyes and looked around the small bed chamber.

Uncle Hiram still lay in the other single bed, his loud breathing steady in sleep.

His chest rose and fell under the heavy quilt that covered him, concealing his bandaged arm. This chamber was much cooler than the main room, chilly enough she could almost see her breath in the air above her. The weather had, indeed, turned quickly, as Mr. Coulter had predicted last night.

She forced herself to move, to push her blanket aside and pull her feet from its warmth, placing them on the icy wood floor. At least its surface wasn't the dirt beneath a flimsy canvas tent, as she'd slept the night before last. And every night for nearly a month now.

A glance at the window showed sunlight through the frosty pain. Her heart lurched. It was too bright.

Had she overslept?

She stepped as quietly from bed as she could, then retrieved her dress from the foot of the bed where she'd laid it out last night. After rebraiding her hair and slipping into her clothes and boots, she stepped through the door connecting their chamber to the main room.

Two women worked by the cookstove, Dr. Coulter and the dark haired woman who was much quieter than the others.

She walked toward them. "I'm sorry I slept so late." A glance at the table showed no food or dishes on it. Had they already eaten and the family dispersed for the day? She was even later than she'd thought.

Dinah sent a smile as she continued scooping something lumpy from one bowl into a larger one. "You must have needed the rest. Patsy and Lillian went with some of the men to help clean Patsy and Jonah's new cabin. Miles and Gil are doing chores in the barn, but I think Miles will be glad to see you're up and feeling well." A sparkle lit Dinah's gaze, and heat swept up Clara's neck.

How silly to let mention of Miles affect her. She forced her mind to focus on what she could do to help. "Is there a broom I can use to clean up?" She'd seen one of the women sweeping around the table after last night's meal. Her stepmother had usually asked her to perform that same task at home. Along with many other chores Sarah found beneath her.

Dinah reached behind a stack of crates and pulled out a broom. "Here it is, but you don't have to work. Why don't you have breakfast while the food is still warm."

It felt wrong to sit and eat while others worked, but Dinah's warm smile and the gurgle in Clara's middle from the rich aromas won out. She settled at the table where Dinah placed a steaming bowl of porridge and a mug of coffee.

The food tasted every bit as good as it smelled, especially the bacon and biscuits the other woman—Jess—brought a moment later. Clara ate with vigor. Normally hunger didn't overtake her this way, but something about this place made her feel like this was the first time she'd had a decent meal in years.

Her thoughts drifted to the day ahead. She needed to ride out to the survey camp and gather enough supplies to make the evening meal for the men. It would be a challenge to transport everything on horseback, but she would manage.

Almost as if reading her mind, Dr. Coulter spoke up. "You know, Clara, you're welcome to use our food stores to prepare meals for the surveyors. It would be much easier than hauling supplies from the camp."

Clara paused, her fork halfway to her mouth. " I couldn't impose like that. You've already been so generous."

The woman waved away her protest. "Nonsense. We probably have a lot more options too. When you're ready to cook, let me know, and we'll all pitch in how ever we can."

Warmth spread through Clara's chest. Why would Dr. Coulter offer such benevolence? It felt like there should be an underlying motive, but what would that be? "Are you certain?"

Jess looked up at Clara and smiled, speaking for the first

time. "The Coulters are sincere in their goodness. I'm often surprised at it, too, but they are simply good people."

Dr. Coulter waved the compliment away, wrapping an arm around Jess's waist. "The problem is, you didn't meet with nearly enough kindness before you came to us. What we have is nothing special."

Even Clara knew that statement to be a falsehood. If only a part of what she'd experienced last night was real—the camaraderie, the laughter, the genuine care for one another—it was more than she'd known in a long while. Perhaps ever. The sense of family and belonging here was palpable, and it tugged at something deep inside her. She swallowed past the lump in her throat and focused on her meal. She couldn't allow herself to get attached. Doing so would make leaving that much more difficult.

When she finished eating, she washed and dried her dishes. Jess sent her a smile of thanks when she handed over the clean plate and spoon, then Clara reached for the broom. Sweeping was something she knew well.

By the time she brushed the last bit of dirt out the front door and replaced the broom in its spot behind the crates, Jess had gone to the barn to see Gil. Dinah sat at the table, studying a large book.

Clara cleared her throat. She hated to interrupt her reading, but she should at least decide what she'd cook for the meal tonight to know how long she would need to prepare. "I suppose I should start planning the evening meal for the surveyors. If you're sure it's no trouble to use your supplies?"

Dinah waved away her concern. "It's no trouble at all. Let's see what we have that might suit a hungry crew of men."

After Dinah showed her their substantial supplies, they chose a ham and potatoes to bake. Fresh sourdough bread would go well with that, and if she cooked enough of everything, the men would enjoy leftovers tomorrow morning before they headed out to work.

Dinah touched her shoulder as she stepped back, allowing Clara space at the counter. "I'm going to check your uncle and see if he's ready for me to change his bandage."

Clara jerked her gaze to the woman's eyes. "Shall I help you?"

Dinah's expression softened as she shook her head. "No need. It'll only take a minute."

When Dinah left, Clara opened the wooden crock the doctor had indicated held the sourdough starter. The sharp, fermented aroma hit her nose as she peered inside at the spongy mixture.

She found a large mixing bowl and carefully measured out a scant cup of the precious starter, using the edge of her hand to level it off just as Sarah had taught her. Even the smallest excess could throw off the entire recipe—she'd learned this the hard way, much to Sarah's frustration. And she certainly didn't want to deprive the Coulters of more than she had to use.

Next came the flour, poured from a cloth sack into a neat mound atop the starter. She used her fingers to create a well in the center, then slowly added cool water from a pitcher, pulling in the flour bit by bit until a shaggy dough began to form. The repetitive motion of mixing soothed her nerves as much as the feel of the living dough beneath her hands.

Once the dough came together, she tipped it onto the floured counter and began to knead. Push, fold, turn. Push, fold, turn. The steady rhythm took her back to countless times she'd done this in their kitchen at home. She'd taken over most of the food preparations by the time she turned fourteen. Though the work seemed endless at times, she appreciated the challenge of making something tasty with only a few precious ingredients.

Dinah stepped from the chamber Clara shared with her uncle and moved to the wash basin against the wall to scrub her hands. "Hiram has a bit of a fever this morning, but that's normal. His body is working to create new skin over that burn."

Clara's chest tightened as she turned to the woman, though she kept her flour-covered hands over the counter. "Is it bad?"

The doctor dried her hands on a towel. "It's not too high. We'll keep a close eye on him, make sure he's drinking enough water. I might change that bandage three times today. Infection is always a risk with severe burns, but he should recover well. It just takes time."

Clara's lungs squeezed tighter. She couldn't lose Uncle Hiram. Abandoning the dough, she wiped her hands on her apron. "I'm going to speak with him, see if there's anything I can bring him."

Dinah's voice drifted from behind as Clara strode toward the chamber. "I'm making a tea to help with the pain and healing."

Clara could only nod as she pushed open the door. She had to see for herself exactly how bad this situation had become.

CHAPTER 4

*U*ncle Hiram lay much like Clara had seen him less than an hour ago. His eyes were closed like he was sleeping.

But his lids flickered open when her footsteps sounded on the wood floor. He gave her his familiar smile, though it appeared weaker than usual. "Morning."

The chair had already been moved to the side of his bed, so she sank into it. "I hear you're not feeling well today."

He shifted under the quilt. "It's not too bad, just a bit warm and achy. Nothing I can't handle."

Clara touched his forehead. The heat there made her flinch. He felt hotter than she'd expected. "Dr. Coulter says she'll be changing your bandage more often today and giving you tea for the pain."

"Ah, yes. The good doctor has been very attentive." His tired eyes crinkled at the corners. "As have you, my dear. I hope you got some proper rest last night."

"I did." And she loved this place, but did he need more expertise than Dr. Coulter could provide? "Do you think we should go to Fort Benton or a closer town? Maybe a more experienced doctor...?"

He shook his head. "The lady doctor knows what she's doing, far more than many a physic I've been to." He reached out his uninjured hand to cover hers where it rested on the quilt. "Have a little faith, child. The Lord brought us to the Coulters for a reason."

Clara bit her lip. Protesting further would do no good. And she should have the same faith. "You're right, of course. I just...I can't bear the thought of losing you too."

His eyes gentled with understanding. Uncle Hiram was Papa's brother, but he'd loved Mama like a sister. He remembered how hard her passing had been. Though Clara had only been seven years old, she remembered those big tear drops rolling down his cheeks at her graveside. "I'm made of tougher stuff than a little burn. It'll take more than this to steal me from you." His smile held more certainty this time. "Now, tell me, what are your plans for the day? I know you won't be content just sitting at my bedside."

~

*M*iles pulled the front door closed behind him and stepped into the main house, making sure it latched so no drafts would follow him inside. Warmth rushed over him from the crackling fire, and he unfastened the buttons on his coat while he scanned the room. Dinah was working at the cookstove stirring something in a pot. Had Miss Pendleton still not come out?

As he hung up his hat and coat, the door opened to the room where their guests slept. The lady herself stepped through it, her brow lined with worry. She wore a pretty green dress this morning. An apron circled her narrow waist. Was she just now rising? From her expression, something wasn't right.

He moved toward her. "Morning. What's wrong?"

Her mouth pinched. "My uncle seems worse. He's feverish now."

Miles glanced at Dinah, who met his gaze with a reassuring nod. "I've already been in to change his bandage. This tea should help bring the fever down—it's willow bark and garlic."

He wrinkled his nose. Poor Mr. Pendleton. That bitter concoction would be hard to swallow. But if anyone knew how to doctor a man, it was Dinah. Seemed she was doing all that could be done for now.

Miss Pendleton still looked agitated, her fingers twisting her apron. Maybe what she needed was a distraction, something to occupy her mind. Fresh air and activity usually helped, if he could talk her into it.

"Have you eaten yet?" he asked.

She nodded. "I have."

"Well then, why don't you come out to the barn with me for a bit? I could show you the new pickax I've been working on. Or we could check the horses if you'd like."

She hesitated, glancing back at her uncle's door. Then she looked to Dinah, who gave a nod and a small smile.

With a sigh, Miss Pendleton untied her apron and hung it on a peg. "I suppose a few minutes wouldn't hurt. The dough needs to rise anyway." Grabbing her coat, she followed him out into the icy morning air.

As soon as the cold breeze hit her face, her shoulders seemed to relax a little. She took a deep breath, some of the color returning to her cheeks as they walked down the slope toward the barn.

He held the door open for her, and she stepped into the shelter of the building.

Inside, the rich scent of hay and horses enveloped them. Miss Pendleton moved first to her own horse, stroking the mare's nose and murmuring softly. She made her way down the row, petting her uncle's horse, then Miles's own gelding and Gil's mount. Finally, she paused to watch the milk cow chew hay at the edge of her stall that opened to the corral.

He couldn't help but admire the picture this woman made, with her neat golden hair and the healthy flush the cold brought to her fine-boned face. There was a gentleness to her, a warmth that drew him in.

Giving himself a mental shake, Miles crossed to his workbench in the corner, running a hand over the smooth handle of his latest attempt at the hinged pickax.

Miss Pendleton followed, her eyes widening as she took in the various iterations of the tool laid out on the scarred wood.

She reached a tentative finger to touch the shining metal blade of the one closest to her. "You made all of these yourself?" Her voice held a note of wonder.

He nodded, trying not to let his pride surge. "I've been experimenting with different designs, trying to find the perfect balance and weight. This one"—he picked up the ax with the smoothed handle—"is the latest."

She studied the tool in his hand. "The hinge allows the blade to swing freely, using the momentum to increase the force of the blow." Her gaze met his, bright with understanding. "That's brilliant, Mr. Coulter. Truly innovative."

Heat flushed his neck. She'd understood the design without him explaining it. Most of his brothers hadn't done that. What an intelligent mind she must have. "Call me Miles. And I didn't actually invent the idea. Saw it in the store in a little mining town. But I'm perfecting it."

Her smile softened. She looked like she wanted to say something more, but instead turned back to the workbench, her fingers trailing over the various tools and scraps of metal. After a moment, she looked away, and her shoulders sagged a little as she wrapped her arms around her middle, staring into the dim interior of the barn. She must be worrying again.

Maybe talking would help. Remembering better days. "Your uncle, have you always been close with him?"

Miss Pendleton nodded, a gentle smile easing her expression. "Very much. My mother was sick most of my childhood, at least the parts I can remember. Whenever my parents would go off to see some new doctor or specialist, they would take me to the farm to stay with Uncle Hiram."

She wandered the few steps to the open barn door, staring out at the winter brown grass around the cabin. "He taught me to ride horses and milk cows and feed the animals. Everything he did, he let me tag along. My favorite times were at Christmas. Uncle Hiram would bundle me up, and we'd go out in his sleigh, the bells jingling with every step of the horse. We'd glide along the quiet roads, waving to neighbors as we passed." Her voice grew wistful and thick. "Then he'd take me across the open fields where there was nothing but glittering snow and crisp blue sky as far as the eye could see."

Miles joined her at the door, leaning against the frame. Their shoulders nearly brushed as they stared out at the winter landscape. He could almost picture it—a younger Clara, pink-cheeked and bright-eyed, snuggled under thick wool blankets as a stately sleigh carried her over the snow. The image made something ache in his chest.

He cleared his throat. "Those sound like wonderful memories. Your uncle clearly loves you."

She nodded, blinking back the glassy sheen in her eyes. "He's always been there for me, no matter what. And now..." Her voice caught, and she inhaled a deep breath. "Now I need to be there for him."

"You are. You're doing everything you can." He hesitated, then reached out to lay a hand on her shoulder, hoping the gesture would offer some small comfort. "And we're here to help. Anything you need. You're not alone in this, Miss Pendleton."

She looked at him, those luminous green eyes searching his. For a long moment, she was silent.

Had he overstepped by touching her?

Before he could pull his hand back, she reached up to cover his fingers with her own. Though cold outside chilled her skin, her touch sent a flare of warmth through him.

"Call me Clara. Please. And thank you." Her voice came out just above a whisper. "Truly. For everything you and your family have done for us. I don't know how I can ever repay your kindness."

He shook his head. "Nothing to repay." He gave her shoulder a gentle squeeze before dropping his hand back to his side. His fingers immediately missed the contact. Her warmth. "Now, what do you say we head back inside? Dinah's probably wondering what's keeping us."

Clara took a deep breath and squared her shoulders, some of that earlier determination returning to her bearing. "You're right. I should get back to preparing dinner." She glanced up at Miles. "Thank you for the distraction. It helped."

"Anytime." And he meant the words with every fiber of his being. No one else had ever caught his notice the way she did. He'd not be opposed to getting to know this woman better.

A new feeling for sure.

~

Clara tied the last knot in the sack of biscuits she'd pulled from the stove, then turned and carried the bundle out of the cabin.

Miles waited with their horses, the rest of their food already secured behind the saddles.

"This is it." She handed the sack to him. The way he'd strapped the bundles appeared much more secure than her own knots, and the last thing she wanted was to lose any of this good food on the way down the mountain.

She mounted her horse and settled in the saddle, taking in the view while she waited for Miles. Rugged peaks towered around them, some already snow-covered, others still green with pines. So much raw beauty. So far removed from the streets of Baltimore. Different even from Uncle Hiram's farm. There'd been a few rolling hills, but no majestic peaks like these.

Miles tugged the tie strap, then lifted his foot to his stirrup and swung into the saddle. "All set?"

She tipped her head toward the path. "Lead the way."

She'd not asked Miles to accompany her. He'd simply said he was coming. But she was grateful. It would have been a challenge to pack all the food behind one saddle without squashing some of it. And finding the camp in the woods might take longer than she'd like. Not to mention the fact that wild animals might be drawn to the scent of the food. The last thing she wanted was to have to use the handgun she'd dutifully slipped into her pocket.

As they left the clearing, Miles led them on a trail down the mountain.

She breathed in the crisp mountain air, relishing the scent of pine and the feeling of freedom that came in this wilderness.

After a few minutes, he broke the quiet. "So, what are the surveyors' plans for this area?"

Clara studied his back as she rode behind him. "Well, they'll be measuring and mapping the terrain, looking for the best route for the railroad. I'm hoping to get their notes with measurements tonight so I can sketch everything to scale tomorrow."

They rode on for another minute before he spoke again. "They're really surveying for a railroad to come through these mountains? Through here? He motioned with one hand toward the wooded landscape.

Maybe the idea of a train invading his family's property didn't sit well with him. Some people felt that way, though others welcomed easier travel back east. "Yes, but all we do is measure and map. It'll be up to the railroad to decide the route they think is best."

"Hmm." His tone sounded interested, but not necessarily upset.

The trees were spaced far enough through here that she could nudge her mare alongside his horse to see his expressions. "Would *you* want the railroad nearby?"

He shrugged, his gaze lifting to the sky ahead. "Not especially. I'm just glad—" He cut the sentence off abruptly.

She studied him, waiting for him to finish. Or explain himself. He didn't seem like he planned to, so she prompted. "What were you going to say?"

He hesitated, then sighed. "I'm glad you're really surveyors for the railroad."

Glad? Instead of...

He glanced at her and, considering his grimace, must have seen her confusion. "My family's been having trouble from a group of miners who stole from us in the past. We've been on the lookout for them. It's a large group with a lot of contacts, and we'd wondered if your surveying was a ruse and you were part of them."

Indignation flared inside her, and she met Miles's level gaze. Nothing in his expression showed any ill will. From his perspective, they could have been nefarious strangers riding across his land, so she should try to rein in her resentment. She took a deep inhale and offered a tight smile. "I can assure you, we're most definitely not part of a mining group come to steal from your family. I've been with the surveyors since Fort Benton, and my uncle worked with them for weeks before that, all the way since they started at the Missouri River."

His posture relaxed. "I believe you."

She blew out a breath. Jericho's rudeness yesterday now made sense. It was a wonder they'd allowed her and her uncle to stay at the house at all. Perhaps only to keep an eye on them. Either way, they wouldn't find anything suspicious about her or Uncle Hiram.

CHAPTER 5

*T*he next day, Miles had to keep his mind on the task at hand, not let his thoughts roam to the pretty lady back at the house.

"C'mon, heifer. You're almost there." Miles fanned his hat in a steady motion as he guided his mount behind the straggler, pushing the animal through the woods to catch up with the rest of the herd in the east pasture.

Jude was already there with the main group, and Sean rode on the other side, following the dawdlers there.

Snow would begin its frigid grip on the mountains any day, and this east pasture gave the cattle a lot more protection from the wind than the north pasture where they'd been grazing.

The heifer lowed in protest but finally picked up her pace, crashing through the underbrush. At last they broke through into the open pasture where the rest of the cattle grazed, their breath clouding in white puffs against the icy air. He was more than ready to get back to the house and a warm fire.

And Clara. He couldn't deny a bit of pleasure at the thought of seeing her pretty smile.

He nudged his horse toward where Jude had dismounted and stared at something on the ground.

"What do you make of this?" Jude's voice crashed through the image of those sparkling green eyes.

Miles followed his brother's gaze down.

A bloody carcass lay in the grass, mostly bones and hide from what he could see at a distance. As his mount joined Jude's, the details came all too clear.

A cow head lay at one end of the body, leaving no doubt what kind of animal this had been. But the carcass hadn't been ravished in the way wolves would have left it. No, the hide had been sliced cleanly with a knife. The legs mostly intact. The innards piled to the right of it.

Someone had butchered their cow.

And it'd been killed so recently that wolves hadn't even come to clean the carcass yet. Today maybe? Yesterday at the earliest.

Bile churned in Miles's middle. Who would have done this? The only strangers anywhere around were the surveyors, and they had no need of meat.

The Salish tribe to the west were the only other neighbors within a few hours. And they were longtime friends. If any of them were hungry, they knew to come to the house. Though in truth, the people were well established with sturdy homes and abundant food.

Had another band come into the area? One who didn't realize—or understand—that cattle were owned by the local rancher, not fair game for any hunter?

He turned to Jude. "You think there's a new tribe in the area?"

Jude gave a "hummph" that sounded more like a growl. "A new tribe of surveyors." He lifted his gaze to scan the cattle grazing to their left. "They're eating our food, aren't they? That's not enough for them? They need our livelihood too?"

Miles could only stare at his brother. "You think they did this? Why would they?" Jude was usually the level-headed one. The brother who thought before speaking and always gave plenty of grace, even when it might not be deserved.

Jude turned to mount his horse. "Who knows why any man does what he does. Afraid their supplies'll run low. Worried about bein' snowed in. Maybe the railroad doesn't give 'em enough to eat decently so they have to poach food along the way."

He settled in the saddle as Sean rode up, but Jude locked his gaze on Miles as he spoke. "I don't know the reason, but I wish they'd asked us first. I'm starting to think maybe Jericho is right. Having strangers on the ranch just causes problems."

Miles frowned as he mounted his own horse. Not Jude too. Jericho had always kept them too guarded from the outside world, but Jude had been more level-headed. Surely, the surveyors wouldn't stoop to butchering one of their cattle without permission. Not after the Coulters had been so welcoming, providing them a place to set up camp and even sharing meals with them.

It didn't make sense.

He didn't really know the men, but he couldn't bring himself to believe Clara would be part of a group who would consider this all right. And whoever killed this cow hadn't even tried to hide it.

As they rode back toward the house, a tense silence stretched among them, broken only by the crunch of hooves on the frosty ground. The trees were spread far enough apart to let them all three ride abreast.

His mind churned through who besides the surveyors might have killed their stock. He finally voiced the only other possibility that made sense. "We should look around for a new tribe that might have come to the area. Maybe ask Two Stones if he's seen anyone."

Jude didn't answer, just kept his mouth in a thin line.

"I'll go ask Two Stones," Sean spoke up.

Jude slid him a look. "Let's talk to Jericho first. It's possible these are Mick's men, planning an attack."

At nearly eight years old, Sean had become a solid hand with the cattle and horses, but he wasn't quite ready to head off on a two-hour ride to the Salish village by himself. Not with so many strangers around—surveyors for sure, and maybe also natives from who knew what tribe.

When they reached the house, Jude and Sean headed to the barn to see if Jericho's horse had returned yet. He and Jonah had been pushing hard to get Jonah's cabin dried in before the first snow. Jonah hoped to live there by the first of the year.

Which meant a wedding would be coming soon, for Jonah surely wouldn't wait long to tie the knot with Patsy once he had a home ready for her. The two of them were perfect for each other, and Jonah deserved to finally have his own house. Especially since the last cabin had been burned down by Mick's men before he could move into it.

Miles dismounted and tied his gelding to the post near the door. He might be riding again soon, depending on what Jericho decided, but he'd like to talk to Clara first.

He stepped inside, the warmth a welcome contrast to the biting chill outside. Clara, Jess, and Lillian worked around the cookstove and work counter. Clara's golden brown hair was a bit darker than Lillian's flaxen braid, but the two looked like they could be sisters, the older teaching the younger.

She fit here.

He swallowed the strange knot that thought created in his throat.

All three women looked up as he entered, but it was Clara's gaze that lit bright enough to capture his focus. She was such a pretty thing. Like sunshine, she brightened everything around her, clearing away the dark worries in his thoughts.

He couldn't help a bit of a grin as he approached. "Something smells good here." The words came out automatically. They were working by the cookstove, after all. But now that he spoke them, a rich, savory scent wove through the air. His belly pinched in anticipation.

Lillian grinned. "Clara's teaching us how to make carrot pie, and we're making enough for us all, the surveyors too."

Miles raised his brows. "Carrots? In a pie?"

Clara's cheeks flushed a pretty pink. "It's a recipe my family likes. I usually just use any foods I have on hand. The carrots give it a lovely golden color and a subtle sweetness. I thought your family might enjoy trying something new."

"I'm sure we will." He met her rich green gaze and lingered there. She had a way of drawing a fellow in.

Jess wiped her hands on her apron. "What brings you in so early? Gil said you were moving a herd."

Reality splashed over him like snow from an overhead branch. "We got the herd settled in the east pasture. But we found something." He hesitated. Should he ask Clara privately? Likely, the others would learn soon enough. Gil would tell Jess, then they'd all talk about it at the dinner table. No need to tiptoe around the topic now. "A butchered cow. Fresh. No more than a day old at most."

Jess's eyes widened. "Butchered? By whom?"

Miles shook his head. "We don't know for certain. Jude thinks..." He glanced at Clara, hating to say it. "He's wondering if it could be the surveyors."

Clara's eyes went wide. "No. They wouldn't do that." Then her brows lowered, like she was thinking through something. "Is there a reason he thinks they did it?" She shook her head, as though clearing her mind. "Not our group, I'm sure of it. We buy our supplies in towns along the way. Besides, I'm cooking for them here, and most of what I'm using is your family's anyway. They're not low on supplies."

That was what he'd been thinking too. "Would they take the meat if they found an animal already dead?"

She tipped her head, her frown deepening. "Surely, they would have come to the house to let you know."

"I guess I need to see what Jericho thinks. Jude went to find him." He glanced at Jess and Lillian. "Have you seen him ride in yet?"

Lillian gave a quick shake of her head. "You're the first one back. I think the rest are all still at the new cabin."

He turned and strode toward the door. "I'll head over. Jude and Sean are probably already riding that way." Since Jericho, Jonah, and Eric were working there today, they'd all be able to meet and talk this through. Everyone except Gil, who'd stayed close to the house and barn for days, not willing to leave Jess. There was too much concern her controlling, criminal father would come after her.

When Miles led his horse down to the barn, Gil met him at the doorway, a pitchfork in hand.

Gil motioned to the trail to Jonah's new cabin. "Jude and Sean went to talk to Jericho."

Miles eyed his brother. "They told you what we found?"

Gil's jaw flexed as he nodded. "It doesn't sound good."

"I'm going after them to see what Jericho wants to do. You coming too?"

Gil shook his head. "I can't leave the house unprotected. I don't trust McPharland."

Miles glanced up to the cabin he'd just left. "The girls could come with us." It'd take longer than he wanted to wait to get horses saddled for them, but he'd do it before leaving the women unprotected.

"I'll stay here." Gil's tone held no sign of wavering. "Have someone ride back and tell me what's happening."

Miles turned and mounted his gelding. "Will do." After everything Gil went through to get Jess free of her father's iron fist and to the safety of the ranch, he couldn't blame him for wanting to ensure she wasn't forced to return to her father's caves.

~

*A*fter a quarter hour's ride, Jonah's new cabin came into view through the trees as Miles pushed his mount into a trot. The others had already gathered, Jude and Sean standing by their horses in the midst. Each man's face held a serious expression, their postures on high alert.

Jude must have shared the news already.

Jericho turned to Miles as he approached, but when he spoke, his words seemed to be for everyone. "We need to search the ranch. All of it. See if there's anyone else on our land besides those surveyors." His voice tightened. "See if anything else has been taken."

Miles's gut tightened. What if more animals had been killed? What if it could be proven the surveyors did it?

God, that can't be right, can it? Surely Clara hadn't brought this threat to them. She wouldn't willingly travel with no-good ruffians who stole from the people who hosted them. He couldn't believe that of her.

Jericho was already assigning sections for them to search. "Jonah and Eric, ride south of the cabin. The entire stretch from the edge of the south pasture up the slope to that rock tower. From the cabin all the way to where the creek cuts through the edge of our property."

He pointed to Jude. "You and Miles go east from the rock tower all the way to the northeast corner, where the north pasture starts. Two Stones and I will ride from there down to the creek and past it to where the surveyors are camping. Report back at the house, then someone can go out and check the eastern slope."

"What about me?" Sean piped up. "You want me to ride the east slope?"

One corner of Jericho's mouth tipped. "I need you to guard the house with Gil. We're putting two men in each spot, so I'll rely on you to be the second fellow there."

Sean straightened. "Yes, sir."

Jericho turned to his wife, Patsy, and then Jude. "Might be good if you all head up to the house with him. Until we know what we're dealing with, we should all stay close."

Dinah looked at Eric. "I'll get Naomi and the children too."

He dipped his chin. "Thanks."

As the others retrieved their belongings and horses, Jude mounted and rode to Miles. "Ready?"

"Let's go." The two of them would be searching the same area where they'd found the dead cow, so they'd be most likely to find another sign of strangers around that spot. Maybe find a trail.

They couldn't overlook anything. Not the scattered ashes from a campfire, not leaves or dirt sprinkled over with blood from a fresh kill, not even a hoof or footprint. They had to find the truth for everyone's sake. His family and Clara's too.

CHAPTER 6

$\mathcal{A}$ chill wind whipped the branches of the pines above Clara. Goosebumps peppered her exposed neck. The ride to the camp was much quieter without Miles at her side. Maybe she should have waited for him to come back from his search with his brothers for the person who'd killed their cow, but Holloway wouldn't want the food to be late. She'd been able to load the meal into her saddle bags, so she'd not needed an extra horse to carry everything.

She guided her horse down the slope to the surveyors' camp, the two heavy pies shifting in her saddlebags as the animal maneuvered a steeper portion of the trail. Miles's brother Jude suspected the survey crew.

But that couldn't be the case. She would have known something to be amiss with the men by now, and they'd never shown a tendency to steal a bushelful of apples, much less an entire heifer.

As she rode across the creek, she squinted to see the camp through the trees. Several forms moved between the trunks. Were the men back already? It was only mid-afternoon. Surely, they'd not stopped working with so many hours of daylight left.

All four of them gathered around the fire, so maybe they'd come back to warm up. As she neared the edge of camp, Mr. Holloway rose and stepped toward her.

She reined in and jumped down to meet him.

"Miss Pendleton," he greeted, his voice gruff but not unkind. "We came back early, hoping to catch you."

She frowned. "Is everything all right?"

He raised his brows. "How's your uncle faring?"

Why ignore her question? She glanced at the other men. No one looked especially upset, just their usual sullen expressions. Except for kind Mr. Goodwin. He didn't smile now, but his eyes looked bright and pleasant.

She turned back to Mr. Holloway and searched for a sign of what he wasn't saying as she answered his question. "He had a fever yesterday, but it's lessened today. Dr. Coulter seems pleased with his recovery so far."

"Good, good." He nodded, but his tone lacked any real warmth. "I wanted to make sure I spoke with you. I have a job for you while you're staying at the ranch."

"Of course." She wondered what he might ask of her. "I have the maps caught up, and I'm ready to take back your notes from yesterday and today so I can add the new details. And I brought food." She motioned to her saddlebag.

Holloway called over his shoulder. "Goodwin, unpack the meal while I speak with Miss Pendleton." Then he motioned for her to follow him a few steps away from her horse. "There's something else I need you to do." His voice lowered as he continued. "Have you had much time to yourself at Coulters'? A chance to roam around the house when no one else is there?"

A tingle crept across her shoulders. What was he about to ask of her? She gave a small shake of her head. "There's always someone around."

Her reply didn't douse the glimmer in his eye. "I'll bet you can find a way to avoid being seen. Even if it's in the middle of the night." His voice dropped a little, forcing her to lean in to hear him. "I need you to find something. A paper Winston said is critical for the railroad. They need it at any cost."

Winston. He was the big boss in charge of the surveyors.

She dared to ask, "You heard from him? Has someone been to town for messages?"

Now Holloway frowned. "No. This has been part of our orders from the start. I need you to find a paper Coulter would have stored in a safe place. A trunk maybe, or under a loose rock at the fireplace where it wouldn't burn if the cabin caught fire."

Her heart thumped as she tried to make sense of what he was asking. "What kind of paper? What's on it?"

"It's a deed. And it's important we get it. If you're not sure what you're looking for, bring any documents you find to me and I'll review them."

Clara could only stare at him. "A deed? You want the deed to...what? Their ranch?" What kind of malarky was this?

The man raised both hands as though to placate her. "It's not for me. Winston said it's vital to success of the railroad through these parts. As important as accurate maps, or maybe more so."

What in earth's name did the railroad want with the Coulters' deed? Or rather, she could imagine what they wanted. The land. But without paying a fair price?

Her jaw had fallen open, but she closed it as a new thought slipped in. "Have you done this with all the other land we've surveyed? Did you steal their deeds too?" Her voice held a tone he might not like, but she couldn't help herself.

Did Uncle Hiram know about this thievery?

He shook his head quickly. "No. There's something special about this one. Something Coulter's doing here that's violated his right to the land. Winston said this is critical." His expression shifted, his mouth softening but his eyes going cold. "Miss Pendleton, I've been authorized to do whatever necessary to obtain the deed. If you can't get it for me, I'll have to find a way to get it myself. If that means I have to eliminate a few Coulters..." He lifted a shoulder and let it drop—and the implication hung between them.

"Eliminate?" Her voice pitched high in a squeak. "What will you do to them?" She should stop asking questions, especially when she didn't want to know the answers. But maybe she could find out Holloway's plan and warn the Coulters.

Holloway's tone dropped, low and menacing. "We'll do what we have to. Pick them off one by one. Maybe starting with that younger fellow you seem to have taken a shine to."

She sucked in a breath. How could Mr. Holloway have noticed anything between her and Miles in those brief moments when they first went to the cabin? Unless they'd been spying on her. They might've done that yesterday when she and Miles rode here to deliver food.

The thought made her skin crawl.

She battled to keep her face impassive as her mind raced. She couldn't let any harm come to the Coulters, especially Miles. And she couldn't betray their trust by rummaging through their home and stealing the deed to their property.

There had to be another way. She needed to buy herself some time to figure out a plan.

Swallowing hard, she forced herself to meet Holloway's cold gaze. "I'll...I'll see what I can do. But I need to find the right opportunity. I can't just go tearing the place apart with them there."

He gave a curt nod. "You have two days. I'll expect you to bring me that deed when you deliver our meals, day after tomorrow." His eyes narrowed. "And don't even think about double crossing me or tipping them off. It would be a real shame if a stray bullet found its way to your uncle during all the chaos."

His words sent a punch to her gut. Threatening *her* was one thing, but to bring gentle Uncle Hiram into this? Tears stung her eyes, but she blinked them back. She refused to give the vile man the satisfaction of seeing her crumble.

"I understand," she bit out. "I'll get you the deed. Just…leave my uncle out of this."

A cruel smile twisted his lips. "Glad we have an agreement. Now, I'll escort you back. Can't have you changing your mind along the way."

A weight pressed hard on her chest as she walked numbly to her horse.

Mr. Goodwin held the animal as she climbed back on the saddle. Did he know about Winston's order to get the deed? Would he help enforce it?

His face held a pleasant expression, nothing menacing. But could she trust it? She'd been fooled all this journey. Now, she couldn't be certain of anything where these men were concerned.

The thought brought up the question she'd meant to ask when she first arrived. A glance at Holloway showed him mounting his still-saddled horse. She aimed her question at Goodwin, but the others would likely hear. "Do you know anything about one of the Coulters' cows who was killed and butchered in a pasture on the other side of their house?"

Mr. Goodwin tipped his head. "Can't say as I do." Was that a hint of a smirk on his face? She could be imagining it, but how could she know for sure?

She turned her horse back the way she'd come, a rock sinking in her stomach. What could she do? Betray the Coulters, or risk the lives of her uncle and the man she was growing to care for?

She flinched as Holloway trotted his horse up beside hers, and the animals settled into a steady walk.

Lord, show me what to do here.

One way or another, she had to find a way out of this impossible situation. The Coulters were depending on her, whether they realized it or not.

～

*M*iles crouched beside the remnants of a recent campfire, the acrid scent of ash still rising up from the black and white dust. He poked at the powder with a stick. No coals glowed still, but the few tracks around the area looked fresh. None of the underbrush had been flattened though. Had someone built this fire, stood beside it for a few minutes, then left? Why?

Jude studied the tracks.

"What do you make of it?"

His brother's brow furrowed as he raised his gaze to scan the woods around them. "These look like moccasin prints. Not boots."

"An Indian then? Why would he light a fire and leave so quickly? You think he just wanted to get warm? Was there only one?" It didn't make him feel any better that he'd been right, or at least closer to accurate than his brothers. The surveyors wouldn't have built a fire here. They had their own camp.

Jude's jaw tightened. "I don't like it. Feels like they were trying to draw attention, maybe lure someone out here."

A sharp crack echoed through the forest.

Miles jerked his head up, every muscle in his body on high alert.

"Was that a gunshot?"

Jude was already swinging up into his saddle. "It came from the house. Let's go."

Miles sprinted to his horse and leaped up, kicking the animal as he landed in the seat and grabbed his reins.

Another shot sounded, then two more in quick succession as

his gelding stretched into a canter, racing behind Jude on the trail back to the barn.

Please, let everyone be all right, Lord.

As they burst into the clearing around the cabin, Gil appeared by the front door. He held a rifle aimed their way, but the moment he recognized them, he lowered the weapon and sent a worried scan around the edge of the clearing.

Miles pulled up behind Jude, keeping a grip on his rifle as he jumped to the ground. Behind Gil, the door cracked open, and two faces peered out, one atop the other. Dinah and Sean. Probably, the others stood right behind them, just as curious.

"What happened?" Jude held his own rifle in a position, ready to lift and fire.

Gil blew out a breath, his gaze still sweeping the trees. "I watched from the barn so I could see if anyone approached the house. A man crept out of the woods over there." He motioned toward the tree line opposite from where Jude and Miles had come. "He was bent low, sneaking toward the house. I called out to him, but he wouldn't stop. Looked like an Indian, and not one I've seen around here before. He had markings painted on his face."

Miles exchanged a look with Jude. The abandoned campfire, the moccasin prints... It had to be the same man. But why would he risk skulking toward the house?

"I fired a warning round," Gil continued, "trying to get him to halt. But he shot back at me instead." Gil shot a look behind him. "Dinah fired from the house, and he took off running."

"Did you go after him?" Jude was already readying to mount his horse.

"I didn't want to leave the house." Frustration laced his tone. "Who knows if he was alone."

His brother was right about not leaving the women and children, but someone needed to track the fellow.

Miles swung back up on his gelding, too, keeping his rifle ready.

Hoofbeats sounded before they could start forward, and they both paused to see the source.

Jericho broke through the tree line, Two Stones a half second behind him.

Jude didn't wait to fill them in, just kicked his horse in the direction Gil had pointed. Miles followed. He'd never had to shoot at a person, but he'd do it if his brother's life depended on it.

Jude kept his horse at a trot across the yard, studying the ground as he went. Miles also scanned the terrain but shifted his gaze up to the tree line around the clearing a few times to watch for movement.

"Ho!" Jude reined in sharp, then jumped from his saddle to study the ground.

Miles had ridden past, so he turned his gelding back.

It took only a moment to see the crimson staining the grass and the leaves of a tiny sapling. The dirt was packed so hard here that footprints weren't discernable. But when Jude stretched a finger to touch the red grass, his skin came away scarlet.

His face turned grim as he glanced back at Jericho and Two Stones riding toward them, with Gil trotting on foot. "Blood. Looks like one of you hit him."

While the others studied that area, Miles turned his horse toward the woods again and scanned the ground as the animal walked. He searched for footprints in the dirt, more drops of blood... Anything the man left behind that could help them.

He found nothing. Not a trace. Even when he entered the trees, where the leaves on the ground should be turned over from the man's steps, no sign remained that anyone had traveled through here.

Two Stones caught up with him first, with the others trailing, including Jonah and Eric, who must've been filled in on the details. They searched each direction for more blood, broken twigs, churned leaves on the ground. Anything.

Yet not even Two Stones could find a sign of which way the stranger had gone. At last, they gathered at the edge of the clearing.

Two Stones's brow had gathered in a troubled expression. "This man knows how to cover his backtrail. He is skilled in the ways of the forest."

"But why was he sneaking to the house? What does he want?" Jericho's voice sounded as tight as Miles's chest felt.

"We found a campfire in the trees below the north pasture." As Miles filled the others in on the few details they'd seen, Two Stones shook his head.

"This does not follow the actions of a warrior. He is not of my people, this I know."

"What tribe could he be then?" Jonah propped his hands at his waist.

Two Stones frowned, his brow furrowed in thought. "I am not certain. But this man, he does not move like a warrior. And he is alone." He squinted. "It reminds me of a man I knew once whose heart had become stone. His father was a Blood, his mother white. Hated by both peoples, he learned to hate all."

A beat of silence passed before Jericho asked, "You think it might have been a man with mixed blood?"

Two Stones shrugged. "I only know this man's actions are hard to explain, as that one's were. Why would he bring harm to your animals and home if he does not know you? He cannot be hungry when the deer and elk are so many."

Jericho let out a long sigh and scrubbed a hand through his hair, scanning the area once more. "I guess we need to post a guard at each house for a while."

Eric spoke for the first time. "Should some of us move closer to the main cabin? Maybe into the bunkroom? That way we aren't as spread out."

"Good idea." Jericho turned to Jude. "There's room for you and Angela too."

Within minutes, they'd made a plan, and everyone headed back toward the cabin. All except Jericho and Two Stones, who would search farther into the wilderness for the man's trail. They had been best friends since Dat and Mum moved their family from Kansas to this mountain. Jericho could track as well as Two Stones these days.

Miles led his horse as he strode back with the rest of the men—and Sean. But halfway across the clearing, Gil halted and spun to face him, eyes wide. "Miss Pendleton. She took the food to the surveyors' camp."

"Alone?" A cold dread tightened Miles's gut. Clara was out there with a hostile stranger roaming the woods. He spun to loop his reins over his gelding's head. "I have to go find her."

CHAPTER 7

 s Miles swung into his saddle, he scrambled to make sense of why Clara hadn't returned yet. What made her leave in the middle of trouble in the first place? She could have waited until Miles returned to help her take food to the surveyors' camp.

"I'll come with you." Jude turned to mount his own horse.

Surely Clara had heard the gunshots too. Wouldn't that have brought her back in a hurry?

A new thought twisted around his throat, cutting off his air. What if the stranger knew about the surveyors' camp? What if he left their cabin and headed straight there? What would the rogue do to Clara if he found her alone?

Miles's heart thundered as he urged his horse into a canter. When they reached the trees, they had to slow to a trot on the steep downhill grade.

Jude stayed close behind him.

Miles's mind raced as he guided his horse through the woods, his eyes scanning for any sign of Clara or the mysterious stranger. The thought of her being alone and vulnerable, with a potentially dangerous man lurking in the woods, made his insides clench. How could Gil have let her go off by herself?

"Miles!"

The sound of his name barely reached his ears over the crunch of hooves on leaves, and he jerked his reins back and spun to see who had called.

Jude halted his mount too.

To the right, a horse stepped from behind a cluster of cedars. *Clara.*

Relief flooded through him, and he turned his gelding that direction.

Another horse and rider followed her out. Holloway, the lead surveyor who'd come to the house that first time. At least she wasn't alone.

She looked frightened as she approached, those blue eyes wide.

"Are you all right?" He wanted to leap from his horse and pull her down into his arms. A crazy thought. An aftereffect of the panic, no doubt.

She reined in before him, her nod tight. "We were on our way to the house when we heard those shots. Is anyone hurt?" Worry turned her eyes darker blue.

"No one except a man who tried to sneak up on the house." He glanced between Clara and Holloway as he explained everything that'd happened so the man would hear this news as well. "You two didn't see anyone, did you?"

Holloway shook his head. "You know who he was?"

"Never seen him." He stopped himself before saying the fellow had looked like a native. Some people had a deep distrust of any Indians, without stopping to find out the person's character. Best keep that detail to himself so he didn't cause problems for Two Stones or his people, who might come to help.

Instead, he eyed Holloway. "Have you seen any sign of strangers around?"

The man's eyes narrowed. In thought? That didn't seem to be suspicion in his gaze. "Nah. We've not run into anyone."

Miles nodded. "We'd appreciate if you'd come tell us if you spot anyone on our land. My older brother Jericho and our Salish friend Two Stones are out looking for this man's tracks, but the rest of us will stay close to the house."

Holloway nodded, then turned his horse toward the camp. "I'd best get back." He looked over his shoulder at Clara. "You remember what I told you."

She nodded, and for some reason, the worry marking her pretty features didn't fade.

As Holloway rode off, Miles motioned for her to ride beside him back toward the ranch. Jude guided his horse in behind theirs.

He'd been quiet through the exchange with Holloway. Miles glanced back at his older brother to make sure nothing was wrong.

Jude gave a nod.

Miles turned to Clara, who looked as apprehensive as he'd ever seen her. Even more than that day when Dinah had first treated Hiram's burned hand.

"Are you sure you're all right?" He kept his voice low. She might not confide in him like this, with Jude right there behind them. Or she might not confide in him at all.

She nodded, biting her lip. She didn't speak. And she didn't look at him, just kept her focus on the trail ahead.

What had happened? Had the gunshots scared her so? Or the thought of a stranger wandering these woods?

All he could do was assure her they'd keep her safe. "We're bringing all the women and children from Eric's and Jude's cabins up to the main house. I think most of them will sleep in the bunk room, so you won't be crowded in the cabin. This way we can keep everyone safe. We'll have a man standing guard at all times, on a regular schedule. We'll make sure nothing happens. You and your uncle will be safe."

She finally looked over at him and nodded. Something in her eyes pleaded with him. But for what? Safety? He'd just promised that, but he could say it again, a bit more firmly.

"You'll be safe, Clara. I promise. I won't let anyone hurt you. You have the entire Coulter family determined to protect you."

A flash of something—panic? sorrow?—swept through her gaze, but then it was gone. She turned back to face the trail ahead.

What now, God? What am I not seeing? Show me.

~

Clara crept through the darkened main room of the cabin, her stockinged feet silent against the wooden floorboards. Low flames still flickered in the fireplace, casting shifting shadows on the walls. Hopefully, their glow would be enough for her to see without lighting a lantern.

The house had been brimming with people all evening, women and children and men, coming back and forth between this cabin and the bunkhouse and barn. She'd not had a chance to search for the deed with so many eyes watching.

She'd thought about possible places they might hide such an important paper though. This large room couldn't hold many spots. The cooking area didn't seem likely, and there weren't many trunks and storage crates in the rest of the space. One box held toys for the little ones. Two crates stacked on their sides like a bookcase were lined with rows of leatherbound books. A trunk stored blankets and scarves and gloves. No one would keep critical documents in any of those.

The hearth might just be the spot. Tucked in between loose stones, a paper would likely be safe even if the cabin burned down.

She crouched by one end and gripped the rock on the corner, then wiggled it. The piece held solid. Working her way along the hearth, she tested each stone in turn. None budged. She sighed, frustration building in her chest. Where else could it be?

She pushed to her feet and glanced around the room once more. Her own chamber held nothing. She'd already done a brief search before Uncle Hiram went to bed that evening. It was possible the deed could be hidden in the loft, but it seemed more likely to be stored in the remaining bed chamber—Dinah and Jericho's room. She would have to find a way to search it tomorrow. Maybe she'd find a time when the family was outside for one reason or another.

For now, since she was up, she might as well attend to the personal detail that wouldn't be denied—at least not all the way until morning.

She pulled on her coat and wrapped it tight, tucking her chin into the collar. They'd left the latchstring out on the front door in case anyone from the bunkhouse needed to come into the cabin in the night. One of the men was standing guard in the barn. She didn't know the schedule, but he probably saw her slip out the door and trudge through the night's freezing wind toward the corner of the cabin. The outhouse sat behind the main structure.

There had been a nearly full moon before she went to bed, but now clouds covered the light, making the night far eerier than she'd expected.

As she turned the corner, she collided with a solid form.

A scream tore from her throat as she tried to jerk back. But strong hands gripped her shoulders.

Her heart raced, and she struggled against her captor.

"Clara?"

His familiar voice broke through her panic, but her body

took another moment to stop fighting. Her pulse hammered through her ears, and trembling began to take hold.

"Clara, it's me. Miles. Is something wrong?" He still gripped her upper arms, but now he turned so her side tucked against his chest.

She had to pull herself together. Once she could breathe again, she straightened, inhaling to steady her shivers. "What are you doing out here?" Truly. Why was he creeping around corners in the dark, scaring her out of her wits?

"I'm on guard duty." He loosened his hold but didn't let her go completely. "I was just walking around the back of the house to check things out."

Of course he was. "I thought the guards were watching from the barn." Now her teeth had begun to chatter, probably as much from nerves as cold.

"I was. But every so often I walk around the clearing to see behind the house. Let's get you back inside. You're freezing."

She pulled away from him. "I need to visit the privy first."

A second passed, and she couldn't see his expression for the shadows. "All right. But be careful." The worry in his voice couldn't be denied.

But her business also wouldn't wait, so she bolted for the little shack behind the house.

CHAPTER 8

*M*iles watched the outhouse door as he tucked closer against the cabin wall to block out more of the wind. How had it gotten this cold so quickly tonight? The clouds covering the moon looked like snow clouds. Probably, tomorrow the first flakes of the season would drift down.

He'd like to be inside, stoking the fire and warming the tea Dinah had left for the night watch. But he'd couldn't leave Clara out here alone. He couldn't take that risk with her. Especially after he'd scared her so badly when she rounded the corner.

He'd heard her footsteps and tried to make his presence known before she reached the end of the cabin. But he'd not been fast enough. As good as it'd felt to have his arm around her, knowing he'd caused her fear more than cleared away any pleasure.

Finally, the outhouse door opened and she stepped out. He moved away from the shadow of the cabin wall into the faint moonlight so she could see him well.

Clara startled slightly when she caught sight of him, but then visibly relaxed. She drew her coat tighter around her, hurrying toward him, her breath forming clouds in the frigid air.

When she reached him, she slowed. "You didn't have to wait for me."

He motioned for her to walk past him. "I didn't mean to scare you before. Let's get inside where it's warm."

As they reached the front of the cabin, a faint mournful wail sounded in the distance. He froze, straining to listen. Was that a wolf howling, or a human sound?

Clara must have heard too, for she also stilled.

The noise came again, long and eerie. It couldn't be a wolf, not the way it rose higher instead of dropping lower.

Clara turned to him, her jaw dropping open. She spoke in a whisper. "That sounds like Mr. Goodwin's violin. But how could we hear it this far away?"

A violin?

Again the sound came. *Yes.* That rising cadence did sound like a violin. How could he have missed it before?

Clara still looked surprised, and he flashed a grin. "The air is so thin up here, sound carries when everything is still."

Her expression turned to understanding, and she gave a small smile as she listened to the next series of notes.

She shivered again, then glanced at the door. "We should get inside."

He nodded, then motioned for her to lead the way.

The cabin was still warm from the earlier fire, but he added a few more logs and stoked the embers until flames crackled to life.

She settled onto one of the chairs by the hearth, extending her hands toward the heat. At least she didn't go straight to her room. It would be nice to talk for a few minutes while he warmed up.

After moving the kettle nearer the flames, he poured the last of the clean water into the pot. "That should be enough for tea now. I'll refill it from the wagon when I go back out."

"You have extra buckets of water in a wagon? I wondered how you carry water all the way up this mountain."

His frozen mouth tried to smile, but his cheeks wouldn't budge. "Better than that. A few years ago, I invented a water wagon. It's that big barrel on wheels by the side of the house. We hitch a team to it and pull it down to the creek. I have a pipe that attaches to it to fill the water, then we drive it back up here beside the house. There's a tap on the side to fill buckets from."

Her eyes widened. "I've seen it. You built that?"

He nodded, hoping the pleasure at her praise didn't show as he poured mugs of tea for each of them. "It was a fun project to design. Something that would make life easier for everyone."

She gripped the cup he handed her in both hands, holding it close to her chin so the steam rose up to warm her face. She was so pretty, so alive with those blue eyes bright, even in the shadows. "That's really clever. Have you made anything else?"

He did his best to push down the flush of pride as he settled into the seat beside her. "A few things. They haven't all worked out as well as I wanted."

He paused as memories of past failures rose up. Maybe sharing one would help her feel more at ease. Maybe then she'd be willing to tell him what had made her so scared earlier today when he'd found her with Holloway. Which story should he tell? Something innocent? Or the one that turned out the worst? In for a penny, in for a pound, as they said.

He extended his feet out in front of him so the fire could warm the leather of his boots. "Well, there was the time I tried to rebuild a wagon wheel. I had just learned how, and Dat asked me to replace some broken spokes on a rig he'd bought off someone passing through. I worked real hard on making those new spokes, fitted them just perfect and tight. But Dat told me to check the other spokes too, the ones already there. I didn't take much time with that, looked at one and figured the rest were fine."

He shook his head as he stared into the flickering flames. "A few days later, Mum was driving that wagon full of hay down to the west pasture. Halfway there on the rocky trail, two of the old spokes gave out, just snapped off. The wheel couldn't bear up under the strain, and it flattened, then split off the axle. She was stuck out there alone. I'm thankful the trail wasn't steeper, because the wagon could have easily tipped." Familiar shame crept back through him. "She could have died because I didn't spend enough time to see that the wood had weakened."

Clara was watching him, her expression hard to read. "That must've been hard, realizing your mistake put your mum in danger."

He liked that she didn't try to give him meaningless reassurances like his big sister Lucy had. It sounded like Clara understood, maybe even knew how that kind of mistake felt. "Dat was nice about it, though I could tell he was mad. You can be sure beyond a doubt, though, I've learned my lesson. Anything I work on gets checked completely. I know how quick this land can take a life. I won't let that happen because of something I didn't do right."

She offered the same stiff smile. "I know what you mean." Her gaze shifted to the fire, as though her own memories were taking over her thoughts. Maybe if he gave her time, she would share one.

After a moment, she spoke, her eyes still locked on the leaping flames. "My mama died of consumption. She first became ill when I was little. A year or two old maybe. But it didn't get bad until I was six. Papa took her to every doctor they could find who specialized in lung ailments. All up and down the east coast." She glanced at him. "That's when I stayed with Uncle Hiram so often."

He nodded. "I'm glad you had him. That must have been a hard time." His own parents had died quickly, within a week of taking sick with the fever. Losing them had been such a shock.

Would it have been easier if he'd had more time to realize how ill they were? More time to say goodbye?

More time to watch them suffer and wither away? Maybe not.

Clara sipped her tea, the dancing flames reflecting in her eyes. "It *was* hard. I knew Mama was sick, and I was scared. Especially when they'd be gone for a long time. I always feared Papa would come back and tell me Mama had died, and I hadn't gotten to say goodbye to her."

She inhaled a breath that lifted her shoulders, then continued in a softer voice. "But Uncle Hiram was wonderful. He taught me so much during those years. About the land, about the animals, about..." She paused, her throat working as she swallowed. "About how to be strong when everything feels like it's falling apart." Her voice quivered on those last words, but didn't break.

Was that how she felt now, as if everything were falling apart? He and his family had been good to her, hadn't they?

"A few months before the end, Mama was taking a new kind of medicine. A brown syrup in a brown glass bottle." The way she gave those details made his middle clench. What had happened?

Her mouth pressed tight. "Papa worked every day he could. His job is at an upholstery mill, and I think he must have been in trouble already for being gone so long on their most recent trip. He told me exactly which times she was supposed to take the medicine. He showed it to me, there on the counter, set apart from the other glass bottles—the other tonics she'd tried that hadn't helped, and some that had made things worse."

The knot in his belly twisted tighter. "He expected you to be in charge of giving your mother medicine? How old were you?" That was far too much responsibility for a young child. Even one who'd probably matured beyond others her age.

"I had just turned seven, but I wasn't in charge exactly. He just hoped that I would help Mama remember. The laudanum she took made her sleepy. If she didn't wake up at the right time to take her dose, Papa asked me to help her remember."

Still…a seven year old responsible not just for herself, but for tending her ill mother. "Was anyone else there with you?"

She shook her head. "I've never had brothers or sisters." She looked at him, a wistful look in her eyes. "I can't even imagine what it's like in such a big family. You have—what?—five brothers?"

He nodded. "Yep, all older than me and as overbearing as you can imagine. And a sister. She died a few years ago. That was when Lillian and Sean came to stay with us."

She gave an open-mouthed *ahh* of understanding. "I'd wondered whose they were."

"Yep." He'd have to tell her Lucy's story another day. For now, she hadn't finished the tale about the brown liquid in the brown bottle. He could lighten the mood a little though. He kept his expression solemn. "I'd be happy to give you all the brothers you want. Up to five. You just tell me how many."

That brought a full smile to her mouth and softness in her eyes. "I'll have to consider it." Her lips settled into a straight line as her gaze turned distant again. "Anyway, I watched the clock carefully every time Mama laid down for a nap. I could tell she tried to be up with me as much as she could. She was so weak, though. So thin, and she coughed all the time. Always carried around a handkerchief that was usually spotted with blood."

He could see the picture Clara described. How hard it must have been for such a little girl to watch her mother suffer like that?

"One day while Mama was sleeping, I'd brought in a cat that liked to come by and eat scraps. Mama usually fed her on the back step, but I was lonely and wanted company. It was cold outside, too, if I remember correctly."

She took a deep breath, her fingers tightening around the

mug. "I was playing with the cat in the kitchen, and she jumped up on the counter. I tried to catch her, but she knocked over the bottles of medicine. Mixed them all up. I thought I knew which was the right bottle to take Mama when it was time to wake her for her dose. A brown glass bottle with brown syrup inside."

His insides clenched as she continued the story. Like he was a scared rabbit on the path of a herd of stampeding buffalo. There was no way he could stop the awful ending he could see coming.

"Mama was so proud of me for waking her and bringing the right medicine. I can still remember how special I felt, fixing what the cat had messed up. Remembering to wake Mama at just the right time. Taking care of her. But just moments after she swallowed the spoonful, her eyes went wide." Clara's voice rose in pitch. "I panicked. Especially when her face turned white as new snow and she grabbed at her throat. The terror on her face…" Clara pressed a hand to her chest. "I can still feel that dread."

She was quiet a long moment. Was it too hard for her to finish the story? Surely, her mother hadn't died right then.

He could finally bear it no longer, so he prompted her gently. "What happened?"

She blinked. "She hurried to the kitchen and poured some kind of black powder into her mouth. Then she cast her accounts all over the basin. And the floor." Were Clara's eyes turning glassy? "I thought I'd killed her. She was so weak all that day. When Papa came home, I could tell by his worry that the situation was as bad as I thought."

"Did she recover, though? From that wrong medicine? What was in it?"

She gave a half shrug. "I don't know if he ever told me the name of the stuff, but Mama had reacted to it the first time she took it, which was why she had that black powder on hand. She didn't die that day, thankfully. Later, Papa assured me I didn't hasten her death. I suppose she might have been already near the end, but I don't think she got out of bed much after that. Papa had a neighbor come and stay with us the next day. Soon enough, Mrs. H was coming every day, those last few months."

Silence settled over them as he let himself imagine how hard it must have been to watch her mother die, little by little. To wonder if that awful mistake had been at least partly to blame for her mother's strength failing. It sounded like the end had been coming anyway, but a seven-year-old girl wouldn't have been able to reason so clearly.

He wanted to touch her. To reach out and say how sorry he was for all she'd been through.

But before he could speak, she straightened. "Well." Her voice turned brighter. "I didn't mean to dampen our spirits. I only wanted to say that I understand how easily one mistake can be disastrous." She took another swallow of her tea.

He did the same. The liquid had cooled more than he'd expected. He should get back outside and do another circuit.

She pushed to her feet. "Thank you for the tea. And the company. I'm sure I'll sleep better now."

He stood and took her cup, then returned them both to the side of the hearth. "G'night, Clara." Her name rolled off his tongue in a melody that caught him short every time he spoke it.

"Goodnight, Miles." When she said his name in that gentle voice, the sound reverberated through him. He wanted to call her back. To ask her to sit with him a little longer. He'd never felt so…connected to a woman. So seen by her. So drawn to her.

Yet she would be leaving soon. Maybe he should guard his heart. This entire situation was unexplored territory for him. And the last thing he wanted was to find himself scarred by the time she left.

CHAPTER 9

*C*lara peered through the cabin window at Eric playing with the two girls and Sean in the snow, the picture of joy.

Miles had been right about flakes beginning to fall today. They'd started not long after the family finished the morning meal.

Some of the men had left right after eating to crack ice on the creeks for the stock and fork hay from the storage barns in the pastures, but the rest of the group stayed close to the house. They all kept a wary eye around the edges of the clearing for any sign of the stranger, but nothing unusual had happened yet today.

Now, a thin layer of white covered the ground, enough for little Mary Ellen, Anna, and even Sean to laugh and shout with Eric as they made snow angels and snowballs.

She'd done all those things with Uncle Hiram as a girl when she stayed on his farm.

As though her thoughts had summoned him, soft footsteps sounded behind her, and the familiar scent of her uncle filled her senses.

She turned to smile at him, and he wrapped his good hand around her shoulders as he joined her at the window.

"My, they're having fun." His warm voice always sounded like it held a smile. "You should go out and show them a thing or two about how to throw a proper snowball."

She chuckled, leaning into his embrace. "I'm not sure I remember how to make a proper snowball. It's been a long time since we played in the snow together."

He gave her shoulder a squeeze. "Nonsense. Once you learn, you never forget."

The smile stayed with her, even as her thoughts wandered to the barn beyond the playing children. Miles had gone out there a while ago, when she'd been cutting potatoes into the stew to take to the survey camp later. Was he working on his pickax, or another project?

She needed to add the measurements and sketches Holloway had given her yesterday onto her map. Maybe she could take that task to the barn and draw while Miles worked.

How easy it had been to confide in him last night. Maybe because of the darkness. But it was more than that. Miles was simply comfortable to talk to. He listened. Asked questions. Didn't interrupt, but didn't let her fade into silence either. He made it so simple to share the parts of herself she usually kept walled off.

He felt like a true friend, the first she'd had in ages.

And Holloway wanted her to hurt him and his family.

How could she do that? How could she steal the deed to their ranch? Their home and livelihood?

She couldn't. No matter what Holloway threatened, she couldn't do it to these good people. To Miles, her friend.

"I guess I should go catch up on my maps. I might take them out to the barn where there's a bit more space to work."

She didn't miss the twinkle in Uncle Hiram's eye when he pulled his arm back. "Sounds like a good idea, my dear."

Did he know Miles was in the barn? She'd not thought he would think about that detail, but his twinkle said otherwise. Surely, he wasn't trying to encourage an attachment between her and Miles. They would be moving on in a week or two. Whenever Dr. Coulter approved his leaving.

The thought tightened her chest. She'd lost all respect for Holloway, and the idea of traveling on with him soured.

But another notion rose up to fight against it. Leaving might be a good thing. If she could hold off Holloway long enough, they would have to move to the next area to survey, and she wouldn't have to find the Coulters' deed. Could that work? Maybe not, but she would certainly try it.

After gathering her sketchbook and pencil from their chamber, she tugged on her coat and scarf and stepped outside.

The crisp winter air nipped at her cheeks as she made her way down the snowy hill, her boots crunching with each step.

"Come see my angel, Miss Clara!" Anna waved her over to where she and Mary Ellen were playing.

Clara diverted her path to join the children.

Anna and Mary Ellen's pink cheeks nearly glowed against the white snow as the girls displayed their artwork, complete with pebble eyes.

"Those are the prettiest snow angels I've ever seen." She plopped a hand on each girls' knitted cap. "You two are true artists."

"Mine has curls like my Aunt Patsy." Anna grinned almost shyly, revealing a missing front tooth.

Clara's heart melted a little at the sweet innocence. The girl looked to be only six or seven—maybe even eight, now that she took a closer look at the maturity in her gentle eyes. She could still remember being that age and how big every accomplishment had felt.

She leaned down and propped her hands on her thighs so

she was Anna's height. "Your aunt is beautiful, and so is this angel."

Anna beamed, her mouth parting wide enough to reveal a second missing tooth on the bottom. Clara couldn't help wrapping an arm around the girl's shoulders for a side hug.

After another minute admiring their designs, she turned back toward the barn, slipped inside, and breathed in the rich scent of hay and horses.

Miles hunched over his work table near the window, brow furrowed in concentration as he tinkered with what looked like a rifle.

He glanced up at her arrival, a warm smile lighting his face. "What brings you out here?" His rich baritone wrapped around her like an embrace.

Heat crept up her neck. A silly reaction. She wasn't usually shy. "I needed some air, and I have maps to catch up on. I thought it might be nice to work out here."

He gestured to a barrel at one end of his work table. "I'd welcome the company." He moved the few tools away from that spot and swept wood scraps off the surface with his hand, dumping them into a bucket by his feet.

She settled on the barrel and flipped open her sketchbook, but then focused on what he'd been working on. "Are you making a gun?"

He shook his head. "Repairing an old rifle. The firing mechanism was damaged, so I'm replacing that. And the stock has seen better days." He ran a hand over the worn wood. "Once I sand out these nicks and refinish it, it'll be good as new."

She watched his large hands as he worked, strong and sure in their movements. "You're very skilled. Is this something you do often?"

Miles nodded, a hint of pride in his eyes. "I've always enjoyed working with my hands, figuring out how things work and fixing them."

"I think it's wonderful. To be able to take something broken and make it whole again—that's a gift."

"I suppose so." He glanced at her sketchbook. "Though I imagine you know a thing or two about creating beauty from a blank page."

She ducked to hide a blush. "I don't know about that. My drawings are more for practicality than beauty."

"May I see?" He gestured to the book.

She hesitated. The maps would be seen by plenty of railroad employees, but those people didn't know her. Letting Miles glimpse this part of her felt...personal. But she was safe with him. She handed over the book. "These are the areas we've surveyed so far. They'll be added to the official maps later."

As he studied the drawings, his eyes brightened. "These are incredible, Clara. You have a real eye for detail." He traced a finger over a sketch of a rocky outcropping. "I feel like I'm standing right there."

Something released in her chest, easing the tension, lightening the weight there. He might just be kind, but the admiration in his eyes didn't look feigned. "Thank you."

After studying several pages, he handed the book back to her. "I won't keep you from working, but I'd love to see more later, if you don't mind."

"If you'd like." She took the sketchbook and settled on the barrel, then opened to the page where she would map out the notes from the men.

As Miles returned to his repairs, she tried to focus on reading the dimensions and scribbled images of the landscapes that had been measured. But her gaze shifted up to watch him more often than it should. The surety and skill of his hands as he disassembled the rifle. The furrow of concentration between his brows, the satisfied set to his shoulders when a particularly tricky bit went well. He poured such care into the task, such devotion. Like he did with everything.

This ranch suited him, working in this barn. It was hard to imagine him anywhere else. Certainly not back in Baltimore, and not in one of the raucous mining towns either.

"Do you like it here?" The question slipped out before she could stop it. "Living here on the ranch, I mean."

He glanced up, a smile playing on his lips. "It's a good life. Hard work, but rewarding." He set down the rifle piece he'd been cleaning. "We haven't always been here though. Moved from Kansas when I was about six."

"Do you remember much from before?"

He shook his head. "Not a lot. Flashes, mostly. Mum's laugh, Dat teaching Jericho to whittle."

Then the corner of his mouth crooked up. "I do remember the first time we met Two Stones, right after we settled here. This Indian boy just walked into the log cabin Dat and the older boys were building. He spoke a few words of English and told us his name, then wanted to know who we were. He stayed and helped work that afternoon, then came back the next day. After that, he was just like one of my brothers."

Clara smiled, picturing a young Two Stones and the Coulter brothers, working side by side. "That's a special friendship to last all these years."

"It is." Miles's expression sobered. "He was a big help when we lost our parents."

The weight of old grief hung in his words. She knew that sadness. It never left, just...changed. "I'm so sorry. How did it happen, if you don't mind me asking?"

He exhaled slowly. "Typhoid fever. It came on quick. Mum went first, then Dat a few days later. Lucy, our sister, got sick too but pulled through."

"That must have been hard, to lose them both like that."

"It was." He looked down at his hands. "I'd just turned seven. Jericho was fifteen and had to step up, take on the role of provider and head of the family. He's done a fine job of it, even with Lucy leaving."

"She left?" He'd said last night that she'd died. That Lillian and Sean were her children.

"Less than a year after we lost Mum and Dat. Lucy met a miner in Missoula Mills and ran off with him." Miles's mouth pinched in a grim line. "Jericho tried to get her to come home for years, but she was too stubborn. She died of smallpox a couple years ago, and Jericho brought Lilly and Sean to live on the ranch."

A knot formed in her throat. This place was not only home to the men who'd built it and their wives. It had become a refuge for two orphaned children.

She couldn't let Holloway or Winston or anyone else steal it from them.

She had to say something, respond to the sad story about his sister. "Were you close to her? Your sister, I mean."

His eyes met hers, a vulnerability there she hadn't seen before. "I wish I had been. I mostly remember tiny moments, just like with Mum and Dat. I was old enough when she left that I should have a lot of memories. It's like I blocked them out."

Her chest ached for him. For the little boy whose parents had both died when he was so young, then his sister leaving. She couldn't imagine bearing all that. She'd only lost her mother, yet that grief had changed her forever.

She laid a hand on his forearm. "You were just a boy. Sometimes, our minds protect us from the things that hurt too much to remember. It doesn't mean you loved them any less."

His throat worked as he looked down at the rifle in front of him. What thoughts ran through his head? The few memories he could remember? Grasping for others? Or was he considering her words?

Had his focus shifted to her hand on his arm? She shouldn't have touched him. Maybe he was in shock at that bold move.

She started to pull back, but he placed his other hand atop hers, wrapping his fingers around to her palm. His calloused skin warmed her skin. Comforted.

"Maybe so." He lifted his gaze to hers. "Feels a bit easier, talking about it with you."

She swallowed. Her mouth was so dry as those warm brown eyes drew her in. Goodness, he was handsome. Every rugged feature coming together to make a perfect whole.

Then he released her, shifting his gaze back to the rifle and clearing his throat.

She pulled her hand away, letting out a breath as she gathered her wits again.

He picked up the gun and examined the stock, running a thumb over the wood. "Anyway, after Lucy left, Jericho threw himself into building up the ranch. We started with just a few horses, then added cattle. It's grown into a good spread over the years."

And she was being ordered to rip this ranch from his family's grasp. She worked for a normal tone. "You've done an incredible job. All of you. I can see your hand in it. This is more than just a ranch—it's a home, a safe haven." One she couldn't let Holloway destroy with his schemes.

Miles ducked his head at the praise, a smile tugging at his mouth. "I probably don't do as much as the others. Jericho says I spend more time tinkering and making things than being a proper rancher." He chuckled, though the sound lacked any lightness.

She shook her head. "I'd say your *tinkering* is one of your finest qualities. It shows your intelligence, your creativity. The world needs more of that." Maybe she'd gone too far with the compliment, but he had to know his brothers' opinions weren't the only ones that mattered. This man was a rare find.

He kept his focus on the cloth he rubbed over the wood.

"You have a way of seeing the best in people, Clara Pendleton." His rich voice wrapped around her name like a caress.

"I just call it like I see it."

A clatter sounded outside, breaking through the moment.

The barn door whooshed open, and Sean halted in the frame, panting. "Uncle Miles! Jericho said come quick."

CHAPTER 10

$\mathcal{M}$iles's heart raced as he leapt up from the work table. "What's happened? What's wrong?"

"There's smoke." Sean sucked a breath. "Hurry."

Miles bolted toward the door, throwing a glance toward Clara as he moved. She wore as much worry in her expression as he felt. "I'm coming."

The snow had tapered to a few scattered flurries. A group gathered up the hill in front of the cabin. He started toward them, but slowed when he realized Clara was trying to keep up.

Dinah and a few of the other women stood with the men ahead, so Jericho must not be worried about them being in danger outside.

Miles shifted his focus to where a thin stream of smoke rose into the gray sky, curling up above the trees to the north.

He reached the group and stood beside his oldest brother. "Any guesses?" He kept his voice low.

"Looks like it's near the north pasture." Worry furrowed Jericho's brow. "And it's the opposite direction from the surveyors' camp."

Sean piped up. "You gonna see who it is?"

Jericho gave a sharp nod and scanned the others gathered there. "Jonah, you wanna go with me? Probably best on foot so we can keep quiet."

"Let me refill my shot bag and I'm ready." Jonah glanced at Patsy, who didn't look eager for her man to walk into danger. He leaned in and spoke quietly in her ear, and whatever he said must have been magic words. She stood a little straighter, her expression shifting to determination. She almost looked like she planned to accompany them.

But she gave Jonah a solid nod. Then he leaned in and kissed her, and Miles tugged his gaze away quick. There was far too much of that happening in broad daylight these days.

His gaze caught on Clara, who was watching him, something like a smirk on her face. One side of her mouth quirked higher than the other, drawing his focus to the spot. Now *she* had lips that might be worth kissing.

The moment the thought slipped in, he swatted it away. She was a friend. Someone he simply enjoyed being around. And she'd be leaving in days. He'd best keep thoughts of kissing tamped down.

Jericho and Jonah strode away through the snow, disappearing down the trail to Eric and Naomi's. That would be the easiest route to the north pasture.

Silence settled over the rest of them, broken when Dinah spoke. "I suppose we ought to head in for the midday meal. It's ready."

Miles glanced at Clara with raised brows. "You hungry?"

"I could eat. And I should pack up food to deliver to the survey camp afterward."

He did not relish the thought of her venturing out, even with him at her side. Too much danger lurked in the shadows of the woods she'd have to ride through. He cleared his throat. "I can take the food. You stay here where it's safe."

Her brows drew together, a flicker of defiance in her eyes. "I can handle myself, Miles. It's my responsibility."

"I know you can." He softened his voice. "But please, let me do this. For my own peace of mind." He held her gaze, willing her to understand.

She hesitated, then relented with a sigh. "If you don't mind. Can you also bring back any new measurements or sketches they have for me?"

"Of course." He forced a smile. "I'll be your official courier."

Inside, the aroma of stew and fresh bread enveloped them. The women had cooked up a feast, as usual. Despite the unease that had settled over the ranch, the promise of a hearty meal lifted some of the tension from his shoulders.

He and Clara found their seats at the long table, surrounded by the chatter of his siblings and their families. As he reached for a slice of bread, his gaze drifted to the empty chairs where Jericho and Jonah usually sat. *Keep them safe. Give them wisdom and bring them back quickly.*

Beside him, Clara ladled stew into her bowl and her uncle's on her other side. Hiram still looked pale, but as he watched his niece the affection in his gentle smile, matched the way she spoke of him.

She was a special woman. Even in the midst of uncertainty, she maintained a quiet grace.

Miles forced his focus back to his own meal. He had to keep his thoughts from wandering down dangerous paths.

As the bowls emptied, Jude said, "I'll go with you to deliver the food to the camp. It'd be better not to go alone." Sitting across from Miles, he must have overheard the conversation.

Relief eased through him. "That would be good. I was going to wait to leave after Jer and Jonah come back."

"Got it."

They finished the meal quickly, and while Clara packed the

food for the survey crew, Miles and Jude bundled up. She handed over the bundles she'd prepared, and he and Jude headed outside to ready their horses. Surely, his older brothers would return any minute. Had they found the stranger who'd built the campfire? Did the man run, and if so, had they pursued him?

When the horses were saddled and the food secured in their saddlebags, Miles waited outside with Jude, Dinah, Patsy, and a few others, scanning the edge of the woods his brothers had disappeared into.

At last, a single figure jogged into the clearing. Jonah.

Miles held his breath as he watched for a second form.

Jericho didn't appear.

He sent a glance at Dinah, who was gripping her skirts with white knuckles, eyes straining. Actually, her entire body strained, leaning forward as though barely keeping herself from dashing into the woods to find her husband.

Naomi stepped beside Dinah and wrapped an arm around her sister's shoulders. Had she been outside already, or had God brought her out just in time to be the strength Dinah needed?

Tension hung so tight in the air that breathing had become a challenge.

When Jonah came close enough to be heard, he called out, "Jericho's fine."

Miles released a long breath, then inhaled clean air. Where was he then?

Jonah stopped beside Patsy, wrapping an arm around her as he addressed the rest of them. "We found the fire, but no one was there. Looked like they'd left not long before we arrived. Jericho decided to hide nearby and wait. See if they come back. We thought it'd be harder for two of us to keep hidden, so he's the only one watching for now. If he doesn't return in an hour, I'll go out and take his place."

Dinah's shoulders sagged with relief, but worry still clouded her eyes. "How long will you watch if the man never shows up?"

"A few hours at most. If no one shows, we'll figure out our next move." Jonah gave Dinah's arm a reassuring squeeze. "Jericho knows what he's doing."

Miles exchanged a glance with Jude. There was nothing they could do to help here, and they needed to get moving if they wanted to reach the creek-side camp and return before dark.

They moved to their horses, and as Miles tightened his girth, Clara stepped from the house with another small sack.

"Here's the bread. Please be careful out there." Her green eyes met his, filled with concern.

Their fingers brushed, and a tingle slid up his arm.

"I will." He forced himself to turn away.

He and Jude mounted up.

Clara stood with the other women, her golden-brown hair whipping in the cold breeze.

Miles nudged his horse forward, Jude falling in beside him. His mind churned the details about the strange happenings on the ranch. The slaughtered heifer. The stranger sneaking toward the house. The smoke.

The surveyors.

A thought slipped in. "Do you think the smoke might be a distraction?" He slid a look at Jude. "Maybe they're trying to lure enough of us away from the house?"

The idea tightened in his chest. With him and Jude gone, and with Jericho staking out the fire, they'd left it down three men.

Jude's frown told Miles he was considering that. "Possibly." He reined in his horse, and Miles did the same, both glancing back the direction they'd come.

"Should we go back?" He hated the thought, especially when he'd promised Clara he would deliver this food for her. She might try to accomplish the errand herself if he didn't.

"Maybe I should." Jude met his gaze. "You all right going on alone?"

That was a better plan.

Jude turned back, and Miles kept his gelding moving steadily downhill, focusing his senses on the sights and sounds around him. All seemed quiet, save the usual chirping of the few birds that stayed in these mountains in the winter.

After a quarter hour's ride, he crossed the creek, and Holloway rose from beside the fire to meet him. It looked like he was alone. What was he doing here by himself?

Miles reined in his horse, dismounted, and started to untie the food bags. "Afternoon. I've brought the food Clara made." The moment her name slipped out, he wanted to call it back. He should have called her Miss Pendleton. This man might not fancy the idea of his mapmaker getting close to the locals.

Holloway's sharp eyes scanned the trail behind Miles. "Where is she?"

Miles handed the sack that held a pot of stew with the lid tied on. "We had a bit of a situation back at the ranch. Thought it best to keep the women close to the house for now." He glanced around. "Where are the others?"

"Working." Holloway took the sack and peered inside, a smile curving his mouth.

Something about the look seemed almost sinister, though the man was surely just eager to eat. Still, Miles's gut tightened. He turned back to unfasten the smaller bag.

"Everything all right at the ranch?"

Miles focused on the leather knot. Should he tell what had happened? Maybe this would be a good chance to ask some questions. "We've seen a few signs there's someone on the land who doesn't belong." He shot the man a hard look. "Someone else, that is." When he had the bread bag free, he carried it to where Holloway was positioning the pot in the coals of his fire. "Where are your men working today?"

Surprise flickered in the older man's eyes. He gestured vaguely to the south. "They're down in that big valley the creek runs through. Got a lot of ground to cover today."

That was nearly opposite from where they'd seen the smoke. "Do your men ever start campfires when they're out working? I can imagine they might have wanted to get warm during the snow this morning."

Holloway fixed him with an odd look, his bushy eyebrows gathering. "Waste time on a campfire? They'd better not. They're hauling heavy chains and equipment, keeps them plenty warm."

That made sense. And Holloway seemed sincere. "All right then." He glanced around the place. "Miss Pendleton wanted me to bring back the measurements and sketches you have for her."

Holloway rummaged through a stack of papers and charts piled beneath a rock on a nearby stump. He gathered a few sheets and slid them into a stack of empty pans that must have been from yesterday's meal. "This is what we have so far." He held out the pans to Miles.

Miles gripped the metal, but Holloway didn't relinquish it, fixing him with a probing look, his eyes narrowing slightly. "Is there a reason Miss Pendleton didn't come with you? Seems she'd be safe enough with an escort."

Was that suspicion or curiosity in his eyes? Guessing the first, he chose his words carefully. "There're strangers on our land. Until we know who they are and what they want, we're going to make sure the women are safe. *All* the women. Obviously, you don't want harm to come to your mapmaker."

The intensity of Holloway's stare didn't waver. " I trust you'll keep us informed. Wouldn't want any trouble interfering with our work out here."

"Of course. I'd best be getting back before I lose the light."

"Certainly." Holloway took a step away, but his eyes remained fixed on Miles. "Tell Miss Pendleton I look forward to her next visit. Her contributions to this project have been… invaluable."

Something about the man's tone made Miles's gut tighten

even more, but he only turned to secure the pans in his saddle bags. Then he swung up on his horse, more than ready to put some distance between himself and the survey camp.

As he rode away, Holloway's gaze bore into his back like a physical weight. A shiver skated down Miles's spine that had nothing to do with the icy wind whipping at his face.

He urged his mount into a brisk trot, scanning the surrounding trees for any signs of movement. All the while, questions swirled. Had Holloway been truthful about his men's whereabouts today? The direction he'd indicated was a good way off from that mysterious campfire. But something in his expressions had been...odd.

Was he hiding something, or had he simply become a bit daft from so many months in the wilderness?

Miles couldn't shake the feeling that the surveying project was somehow tangled up in all of this. He just couldn't see the connecting threads. Not yet.

CHAPTER 11

$\mathcal{T}$he next day, Clara squeezed past Patsy in the narrow kitchen, the other woman's elbow nearly colliding with her ribs. The cabin walls seemed to press in on Clara, and from the pinched looks on the others' faces, she could tell they felt it too. So many people in close quarters for so long had made the air feel a bit stifling.

Outside the frosty window, fresh snow from that morning blanketed the yard, covering the tracks the children had made earlier that morning with their gleeful play. Their joy had long since evaporated, replaced by whines and squabbles as they huddled by the fire, still shivering from the bitter cold.

"Clara, can you stir these dumplings a minute?" Dinah stood at the stove, holding out the spoon. "I need to check on your uncle."

"Of course." Clara guided the metal utensil around in the big pot of white cream. This was their second batch of the day.

Uncle Hiram had been napping for the last hour, probably trying to keep out of the mass of bodies clogging the cabin's main room.

Her thoughts drifted to the note Holloway had sent with

Miles yesterday, tucked discreetly inside a sketch. *I hope you're making good use of your time at the house. I wouldn't want anyone to get hurt.*

She hadn't changed her mind about refusing to find it. Especially not the more she got to know these people. She could never betray their trust and hurt them in such an awful way.

But Holloway wouldn't be stalled.

Was there another way out of this pickle she was in?

With the constant bustle in this cabin, there certainly hadn't been time to search Dinah and Jericho's room, which seemed by far the likeliest place to find a document that was worth so much.

She nearly jumped when Dinah appeared at her elbow. "Would you mind taking this out to Miles?" Dinah held out a basket, a cloth covering its contents.

Clara nodded toward the bubbling pot she was still stirring. "But the dumplings..."

Dinah took the spoon from her hand. "I'll finish up here. You go on and bundle up. It's frightful cold out there."

The thought of a breath of fresh air, a few moments free of these cabin walls, and a chance to see Miles...

She wrapped herself in her coat, hat, and gloves, then carried the basket out into the crisp, cold air. She inhaled, savoring the sting in her lungs. White blanketed the world, the snow sparkling beneath the pale winter sun.

She canned the beauty and...

A sleigh!

It gleamed a rich brown, it was parked between the house and the barn, two sturdy bays harnessed to it. And there, standing near their heads and wearing a wide grin, was Miles.

"What's all this?" Her heart picked up speed as she moved toward him, boots crunching in the snow.

Miles strode forward, his cheeks flushed from the cold. "Thought you might be feeling cooped up in there with the whole lot of us." He nodded toward the cabin. "Jericho and I talked it over, and seeing as there's been no sign of trouble today, we reckoned it'd be all right if you and I took a little sleigh ride." His smile softened. "I know it's not quite like the Christmas rides you used to take with your uncle, but I thought you might still enjoy it."

Tears pricked at her eyes. Not only had he remembered her favorite memory, but he'd worked to recreate it.

Miles took the basket and helped Clara to her seat, then tucked the blankets snugly around her before climbing in on the other side. He'd even placed hot rocks at their feet for warmth.

As they prepared to depart, the cabin door swung open, and Dinah waved goodbye, a knowing twinkle in her eye. She'd obviously been in on the surprise, keeping Clara occupied while Miles readied the sleigh.

"Thank you!" Clara called out, her heart swelling with gratitude.

They set off down the wide, snow-blanketed trail through the woods, tiny flakes stinging her nose and cheeks.

Miles handled the team with ease, just like everything else he did.

He sent her a quick look, and she smiled. "I didn't know you had a sleigh."

He refocused on the trail. "We usually switch one of the wagons from wheels to runners after the first snow." His breath formed clouds in front of them. "Spent the morning doing that and making it a bit more comfortable."

Comfortable. He'd gone to such lengths, just for her.

As they glided through the hushed forest, the only sounds became the jingle of the horses' harnesses and the swish of the sleigh's runners. Flurries fell thicker around them, flakes the size of silver dollars drifting lazily through the air.

She pulled the blanket tighter around her shoulders, savoring the crisp scent of the pines. Being out here, just the two of them, made her think of Christmas traditions. "What does your family usually do to celebrate the holiday?"

His eyes took on a faraway look, a smile playing at his mouth. "The women make all sorts of bows and garlands to decorate the cabin. We bring in a big fir tree from the forest for them to trim. We make hot apple cider, and the ladies cook up all kinds of treats—molasses cookies, peppermint sticks, spice cake." He glanced over at her. "I hope you'll be here for Christmas."

She let herself linger in the warmth of his regard. In the hope of possibly being part of the heaven he described. Christmas was still a week and a half away, though. Holloway would want to move on before then.

And she wanted them to move on long before the holy day. She needed to keep Holloway from forcing her to find the Coulters' deed. The reminder burned in her chest, and she looked away from Miles's smiling eyes.

She couldn't hurt him the way her superiors wanted her too. And if that meant leaving him as soon as possible, she'd have to prepare for the loss. Make herself look forward to it even.

Miles guided the sleigh into a wide open meadow, the mountains rising majestic and snow-capped around them. He brought the team to a halt, and they sat for a moment, the falling snow swirling around them in the breeze.

"I love Christmas." Miles's voice was soft. "The joy in giving to each other. I've been working on a little gift for each person in the family."

The thoughtfulness of this man never ceased to amaze her. "That's a lot of gifts."

He shrugged. "I've been at it for a while now. Making them bit by bit in my spare time."

The way he used his talents to help others—it was one of the things she lo—

No, one of the things she *liked* about him.

She couldn't let herself think the other word, not even in the privacy of her own mind. Not when their time together would be so short.

Miles set the brake and reached for the basket. "Figured this would be a nice place for our picnic. Probably best we stay in the sleigh, though, the way the snow's coming down."

Indeed, the swirling flakes had grown larger, falling thick and fast from the steel gray sky. The wind gusted, sending a shiver through her as icy air found its way past her coat collar.

Working quickly, she pulled out the still-warm dumplings Dinah had sent. How in the world had she found a moment to pack them without Clara seeing?

They started eating, huddled beneath the thick lap blankets as the snowfall intensified around them.

Miles studied the low grey sky as he chewed, then swallowed. "I think maybe we should head back." He sent her an apologetic look. "I didn't expect the weather to turn so quickly."

"Oh." She worked not to show her disappointment. "Of course."

She repacked the food, and Miles took up the reins, turning the team toward home.

Already, the hot stones at their feet had lost their warmth, and Clara's teeth chattered, her body trembling. Wind surged in gusts, swirling the white so, at times, she couldn't even see the horses.

Miles to be feeling the chill as well, his shoulders hunched. One blanket was draped over both their laps, and he wrapped the other blanket around her shoulders before they'd set out.

She lifted the edge closest to him and spoke loudly enough to be heard over the whipping wind. "Do you want to tuck this around you?"

He shook his head. "Too hard to hold while I drive." But he nodded at the seat between them. "You could scoot closer, though."

She did, and though he'd said he didn't want the blanket, she held up one side. "Lean forward so I can wrap this behind you."

He obeyed. He must truly be frozen.

She slipped the cover around his far shoulder, and he leaned back. Then she pressed closer against his side. The heat of his body seeped into her, and she let out a sigh, some of her tension easing. Hopefully, this would help him too.

Yet even with his nearness, she couldn't stop the chattering of her teeth, or the growing numbness in her fingers and toes. The sleigh picked up speed, the frigid wind stinging her exposed skin like needles.

Thank heavens they weren't far from the house.

~

Snow slammed against them in a fierce onslaught as Miles urged the horses forward. They struggled against the battering wind, and he could only pray the animals knew the trail, for he couldn't see past them.

He tamped down the rising guilt. He'd deal with that later. Right now, they had to get out of this storm—and fast.

The house was probably still another half hour at the horses' normal walk, but at this achingly slow pace, they might be out here an hour. Or more.

Should they stop at the storage shed by the mine? It was close, maybe only a quarter mile off the main trail. He couldn't let her know about the sapphires, but only a few crates were left there, and they wouldn't be marked. If she asked, he could just say they were supplies.

Beside him, Clara trembled, even with their sides pressed together for warmth. That made the decision for him.

"We need to get out of this wind." He ducked his chin so his words reached her ear and weren't whipped away by the howling gale. "There's a shed up ahead where we store supplies. We can take shelter there and wait out the worst of it."

Her pale face stared up at him, her eyes glassy, though she seemed heartened by the suggestion.

He shook the reins, urging the horses forward. Then as soon as the break appeared in the trees to their right, he guided them onto the narrow path toward the mine. This was another trail they knew well, though it was hidden from strangers.

The trees closed in around them, shielding Miles and Clara a little from the unrelenting gusts. But the snow fell thick and fast, obscuring his vision until he could barely make out the horses' heads bobbing in front of the sleigh.

Please, let me have chosen right.

The meager protection of the storage shed seemed like their best chance, but now, as the world faded into a swirling void of white, he feared they shouldn't even try to go that far. Should they stop here and huddle under the blankets? The sleigh runners brought the wagon body lower to the ground, so they couldn't take shelter underneath like they would have been able to if it were supported by wheels.

Clara's life was in his hands.

What if he chose wrong?

What if they ended up freezing, lost in this blizzard?

Another vicious shiver racked her, fueling his determination. She needed more shelter than blankets. The shed was their best hope.

Lord, don't let the horses stray from the path.

He could see nothing in front of the animals. What if he guided them into a tree? He needed to lead the way so they stayed on this narrow trail.

He reined in the team, speaking close to her ear. "I'm going to the horses' heads to make sure we stay on the path." He eased the blanket from his shoulders and secured it around her. Then he pushed the other cover away from his legs and jumped down.

Fire shot through his feet when they landed on the icy ground. They'd been numb, but apparently not completely frozen. He gripped the front of the sleigh to keep himself upright as he started toward the animals' heads.

"Be careful." Clara's call followed him through the haze.

He would have turned to smile reassurance, but he couldn't feel much of his face. So he nodded.

The warmth of the horses' breath clouded in the swirling snow. He'd forgotten how much heat an animal could create when working. He took a quick moment to tuck his hands under Jack's mane and crowd close to the animal, pressing his cheek against the thick coat. Maybe he should have Clara come huddle with the horses too.

But she would be far better off in the shed where the wind and wet couldn't touch her. Especially if he could build a fire there. He moved in front of the team, feeling to make sure no trees blocked their next step. His hands met nothing solid, only a wall of white.

Surely, they hadn't reached the clearing yet. Just to make sure, he moved to the left and reached out until his fingers brushed a sturdy tree. Good.

He grabbed Jack's reins and started forward, waving his hand in front of him as he moved. Back and forth he motioned, leading the gelding behind him. Every few steps, he reached to the left to make sure he could feel a tree far enough away that the sleigh wouldn't brush against it.

Their progress came painfully slow, but he couldn't risk losing the trail.

"Miles?" Clara's voice sounded like it came from a long distance, muffled as it was by the snow and wind.

"I'm here." His heart thudded even faster.

"Are you all right? I can't see you. Are you too cold?"

"I'm all right. We're making progress. Should reach the shed any time. Are you warm enough?"

She wasn't. He knew that. But mostly he wanted to know how her spirits were.

"I'm fine. Be careful. Please."

A tiny bit of warmth eased through him. "I will."

As he squinted through the white, doing his best to keep the snow out of his eyes, a dark shape rose up on his left. Was that the gnarled oak? If so, they were only a few strides from the clearing.

Thank You, God!

Relief surged through him, but he tamped it down. They weren't out of the woods yet—and he meant that both ways.

He didn't even have to see the clearing to know when they reached it. The howling of the wind intensified, screaming around them with renewed fury.

He turned the team a little to the left, aiming straight for the shed, or so he hoped. His sense of direction felt askew. Not quite trustworthy.

When they'd gone far enough that they should have found the building, he halted the animals again. Then he took a few steps forward into the white, leaving the team behind. He might be making a disastrous mistake.

But his hands struck something solid. He felt the shape—flat, rough wood under both hands. He moved sideways, groping until he found the corner. This was the direction he needed to bring the sleigh.

When he reached the team again, he yelled back to Clara. "We found it. Let me bring the animals forward, and I'll help you down."

As the horses came abreast of the structure where the team would be protected from the harsh wind, he halted them. "Good, boys." He stroked each animal's neck, murmuring encouragement. Jack and Jerry were good wagon horses. Brothers, though a couple years apart. They would get a warm rubdown and dry stalls once they made it back to the barn.

For now, he returned to the sleigh. The horses had thick coats to protect them from this weather, but Clara didn't.

"Here, let me help you." He reached for her, steadying her as she climbed down from the sleigh.

She landed on the ground, wobbled.

He caught her around the waist to steady her. He knew exactly how much her feet likely stung. He held her close, giving her a minute to get feeling back in her feet.

And relishing the feel of her in his arms, even through the many layers between them.

But he couldn't linger. They had to get inside.

CHAPTER 12

*M*iles led Clara through the knee-high snow to the shed. He fumbled along until he found the door. He undid the latch, then gave it a hard pull. He had to yank once more before it gave, pushing against the piled snow.

He ushered her inside and slammed the door behind them. The only light filtered in through the cracks between boards.

The sudden absence of wind was almost disorienting. His ears rang in the relative silence.

"Th-thank the L-lord." Clara's teeth chattered violently. "I d-didn't know if w-we would m-make it."

"I didn't either for a minute." The activity had warmed him a little. He looked around the small space, illuminated only by the pale light filtering in through the cracks in the walls. Four crates were lined up against the far wall—what remained of their sapphires after Mick's team had stolen the rest. *Lord, don't let Clara ask what's in them.*

"Wait here a moment." He kept his voice low in the heavy stillness. "I'm going back to get the blankets and food and my tinderbox so we can try to build a fire." Thank the Lord they'd added a metal vent hole in the ceiling so they could build a fire to warm up out of the wind when they worked here in the winter.

"All right." Her words came as a mere wisp of sound.

Back in the wind, he squinted against the stinging ice, feeling his way to the sleigh, every movement awkward as his frozen body protested. By touch, he located his sack in the back of the sleigh, then the basket of what remained of their lunch. He grabbed them and the blankets.

Once inside, he pulled the door closed. The silence wrapped around him again, and he exhaled. Now, for a fire.

He handed the blankets to Clara and motioned to the crates. "You can sit there until I get us some warmth."

She did, and he crouched down and rummaged over the debris on the ground to gather fuel—twigs, bits of wood, leaves, pine needles. Anything that would burn.

He found his tinderbox in the possibles sack he'd tucked in the sleigh and set to work creating a spark to light the wool he carried in the case. After a few minutes, he managed to coax a tiny flame to life among the pine needles. It sputtered and danced, so fragile, but finally, it held. He fed in more twigs and needles. The little blaze grew slowly until he dared to add slightly larger sticks.

Clara was huddled on the crate, the blankets wrapped around her, staring at the small fire as if willing it to grow.

"Come closer. You'll warm up faster."

She rose and shuffled toward him, sinking down to sit cross-legged by the growing flames. She held out her gloved hands, letting the heat seep into her frozen fingers. "Thank you." At least her teeth had stopped chattering. Her eyes glimmered gold in the firelight as she looked up at him. "For getting us here safely."

"You're welcome." His voice came out gruff. Maybe cold-roughened, or maybe from the knot in his throat. He should have turned them back sooner, the first minute the wind blew stronger. Once more God had protected someone he cared about from the result of his actions.

He looked away, focusing on building up the fire. "I need to get more wood so we can keep this going a while."

Fear sparked in her eyes. "But…it's dangerous out there."

He laid a gloved hand on her arm. "I'm not going far, just around the side of the building. I'll come back. I promise."

He made his way to the door and slipped outside.

The wind slammed into him, stealing his breath. Snow pelted his face as he felt along the side of the shed, digging through the thick cover to find the driest branches buried beneath. The shed was tucked at the edge of the clearing, so trees lined the back of it.

His hands ached with cold as he snapped off dead limbs, tucking them under his arm. It would take a while for these to dry out enough to catch, but it wasn't as if he had another option.

Back inside, he arranged the branches near the fire, close enough to feel the heat but not so near they would smother the flames. "I think one more load will be enough." The dead wood he'd already found should catch quicker, but it would burn too fast. He needed some greener logs to keep the blaze going a while.

"Can I come help?" Clara's voice sounded small from the back of the shed, but at least her teeth weren't still chattering.

He shook his head as he moved to the door. "We only need the one load."

Once more, he ducked back out into the howling storm, wrenching the door tight behind him. There had to be branches, something he could use to build up the fire.

The wind snatched at his clothes with icy fingers, and he squinted against the swirling snow. He kept one hand on the rough wall of the shed, feeling his way around to the back. Finding larger logs took much longer, but at last he stumbled on a fallen tree that yielded what they'd need for now. He dragged two long pieces back with him.

When he finally stepped back into the shed and secured the door, he dropped the logs and stomped the snow from his boots. His eyes took a moment to adjust to the dimness after the blinding white outside. But when his gaze found Clara, he froze.

She knelt beside the crates, her eyes wide, her face even paler than before.

A sick feeling twisted in his gut. Had she opened...?

"Clara?" He crossed to her in two strides, kneeling before her. "What is it? What's happened?"

She opened her mouth, but no words came. Just a shaky exhale that clouded the air between them.

Dread pooled heavy in his belly as he glanced at the crates, the unmarked lids slightly askew. He looked back at Clara, searching her stricken face. "Did you...did you look inside them?"

A jerky nod. "I'm sorry." Her voice came barely more than a whisper. "You said you stored supplies. I didn't mean to snoop. I just thought...I thought there might be something to help with the fire. Or extra food." Her hands twisted in her lap, knuckles white. "I shouldn't have..."

Miles closed his eyes. This was it. The moment he'd tried not to think about.

If there were any chance Clara could be a permanent part of his life, he would have found the right time to tell her.

But she would be moving on. He'd not intended to let her know about his family's carefully guarded secret.

"It's all right," he heard himself say, his voice distant to his own ears. "You don't have to apologize." He shucked his gloves and reached for her hand, breathing a sigh of relief when she let him enfold her icy fingers in his own. She must have removed her own gloves to open the crates.

He met her gaze, steadying himself with a deep breath. There was no going back now.

"My family... We mine sapphires." The words felt heavy on his tongue. "It's how we've survived out here. We keep it secret because if word got out, there'd be a mad rush to our land and the surrounding wilderness. Miners and prospectors from all over, stripping the slopes bare. We couldn't risk that."

Her brow furrowed as she absorbed his words. "So these crates..."

"Packed with raw sapphires to be shipped back east."

She gave a slow nod, the worry in her brow only intensifying. "This is how you support yourselves. Such a large group wouldn't be able to survive on ranching alone." Her voice began to drop off with those last words, as though she were talking to herself. But then she kept on in that low tone. "This land, it's invaluable to you. This *particular* land. You couldn't just move to another claim."

What was she talking about? Did she expect him to respond to that? He needed to make sure she understood how important it was to keep this secret.

He took her other hand, which refocused her attention on his face. "Clara, I need you to understand how crucial it is that no one else finds out about this. If word spread, it could mean disaster for my family. For our entire way of life here." He searched her eyes, silently pleading for her understanding. For her promise of secrecy.

She held his gaze, and slowly, slowly, the worry lines began to smooth from her brow, though a hint of concern still lingered in her eyes. "Of course. I won't tell anyone." She gripped his hand tighter. "I promise."

The band around his chest eased, and he exhaled. "Thank you." The words felt inadequate for the wave of relief washing through him, but they were all he had.

Silence stretched between them, broken only by the pop and

hiss of the fire. Miles knew he should rise, add more wood to build up the blaze. But he couldn't seem to make himself move from this spot, kneeling before her, her hands in his.

Clara's tongue darted out to wet her lips, drawing his gaze. "Miles, I..." She faltered, her voice barely a whisper.

His pulse picked up speed. The cold had turned her lips a bright red, especially against the pallor her face still held. They looked a little chapped from the wind. He could soothe them. Warm them. Warm *her*.

His gaze lifted back to her eyes. Did she want the kiss as much as he did? Kneeling here, her hands in his, so distant from anyone else, it felt impossible *not* to kiss her. He was drawn to so much more than her looks. Her mind, her kindness, her wit, her spirit.

Her eyelids fluttered closed, his first realization that he'd leaned in. So close.

He released one of her hands and lifted his to cup her cheek. Her eyelids flicked open. He must have startled her, his skin too icy.

"My hands are cold." Yet this gave him access to lose himself in her eyes, those rich green orbs.

Her mouth parted, and her voice came out breathy. "I don't mind."

She was talking about his frozen touch, yet it seemed like she meant more than that. Like she meant the idea of him kissing her.

He closed the last bit of distance, brushing his lips over hers in the gentlest of caresses. She was a treasure, one he wanted to savor.

A sigh slipped from her, a sound that warmed his blood. He returned for more, and she kissed him back this time.

His heart pumped faster as she leaned into him, her fingers curling into the fabric of his coat. He angled to deepen the kiss. His hand slid into her hair, cradling the back of her head.

This kiss, this embrace—it felt like coming home. Like everything he never knew he needed.

The heat of her was thawing him from the inside, spreading through his veins like warm honey. He needed to slow things down.

And take a breath.

He gave her mouth a final aching caress, one that nearly drew him back for more. Yet he forced himself to pull back, to rest his forehead against hers. Their heavy breaths mingled in a fog between them, like that in his mind.

Her eyes blinked open, hazy and unfocused. A look so adorable, he couldn't help but brush another quick kiss. Her tiny whimper made him smile.

He sucked in a gulp of air. He needed to speak. Needed her to know he didn't take what they'd done lightly.

"Clara." Her name out in a reverent whisper, a reflection of how he felt about her. "You're…special."

Her eyes glistened in the firelight. "I feel the same way about you." Her voice trembled a little. "I never expected…never dreamed I would find someone like you out here."

He knew exactly what she meant. From the moment he'd first laid eyes on her, riding in the midst of that group of men, she had captivated him. Her spirit, her strength, her compassion —she was a rare treasure. One couldn't help yearning for.

Reluctantly, he released her and tended to the fire, adding more branches to coax the flames higher. They needed the warmth, and he needed a moment to collect himself before he said or did something he shouldn't. Not yet, anyway. Not until he was certain of her feelings.

When he turned back to her, she had rearranged the blankets into a makeshift pallet and was unpacking the basket of food. The domesticity of it, of her, struck him deep in the chest. What would it be like to come home to her every night? To share a life, a love, with her?

But she didn't belong here. She had grand adventures ahead of her, a bright future far away from this untamed land. He couldn't ask her to give that up, to tie herself to a hardscrabble life on a remote sapphire mine.

But maybe, for this one stolen moment, he could pretend. Pretend that she was his and this cozy little haven was theirs. Just for a little while.

He lowered himself to sit beside her on the blankets. Outside, the wind howled and moaned, but in here, in their tiny bubble of firelight and shared secrets, none of that mattered. They were warm and safe and together.

And for now, that was enough.

CHAPTER 13

Clara leaned against Miles's solid shoulder, his arm tucked around her, the steady rhythm of the sleigh runners gliding over snow filling her ears. After at least two hours of refuge in the shed, the wind had finally lessened enough that they'd decided to brave the ride back to the house.

Pressed close to him, she could almost forget the bitter cold —and the even more chilling secret that hovered over her.

Almost.

Miles's warm breath was on her cheek. "Penny for your thoughts?" His voice was soft, gentle.

She sighed. How could she tell him the truth about Holloway's scheme without risking everything—her uncle's job, their tentative place here, and worst of all, Miles's trust in her?

"Just thinking how wonderful this ride turned out." She forced a lightness in her tone. "In a very different way than I'd expected." At least that much was true. In the shed, talking for hours beside the fire as they ate the remainder of their packed lunch, there'd been a connection, an intimacy, unlike anything she'd experienced before.

Not just that kiss—as heart stopping and absolutely

wonderful as it had been—but the conversation. She would have loved every moment sharing about her life, snuggled against him for warmth, if she didn't have the awful secret taunting her.

She *wasn't* going to steal their deed.

The fact that she'd ever considered obeying the order made it hard to meet Miles's gaze. And even if she didn't take action, the knowledge that Holloway wanted the deed made her guilty. Winston wanted it, and that meant Holloway would do whatever it took to get the document.

She'd been deceiving herself to think she could hold him off until they rode away. When Holloway realized she wouldn't get the deed for him, he'd find another route.

She needed to warn Miles.

But what would that do to his opinion of her? It would start trouble between his family and the survey team.

Would the Coulters throw her and Uncle Hiram out? With the weather so bitter cold, and after betraying Holloway, where would they go?

Regardless of all that, she *had* to tell Miles. It was the right thing to do. She'd almost worked up the nerve to give him her news right after he told her about the sapphire mine.

But then he'd looked at her with those eyes, those beautiful, love-filled eyes—

And yes, what she saw in them was far more than friendship. Far more than passing affection.

She'd been swept away.

So she'd allowed herself this one afternoon to try to forget about deeds and orders to steal from innocent people. To just enjoy time with this man she was falling for. To be the center of his attention.

When he talked about his ranch, her guilt ratcheted up, so she'd done much of the talking, sharing her own stories. About her stepmother and what life had been like after Sarah came into their home. Clara's days had been easier in some ways, as her father didn't expect her to do things she had no idea how to accomplish as a nine-year-old. Yet Sarah's presence made life harder in other ways. Especially when Sarah got frustrated with living on such a small income and purchased things she knew they couldn't afford.

It felt good telling Miles about her life. She'd never shared those details with anyone, not friends, not even Uncle Hiram. But Miles felt safe. As safe as her uncle, and far more handsome.

The ranch house came into view through the swirling snow, windows glowing with warm lamplight.

A knot twisted in her middle. She had to find a way to warn Miles about Holloway's intentions, without revealing the role she'd almost played. But the thought of losing Miles's trust, of seeing disappointment—or worse, disgust—in his eyes when he looked at her... It made her want to stay hidden away in this sleigh forever, cocooned in his solid warmth.

He halted the horses in front of the cabin, and she eased herself away so he could climb down. The cold assaulted her without his nearness, but he jumped to the ground and reached up to help her descend.

His gloved hands wrapped around her waist, steadying her as her feet hit the snow-packed ground. For a fleeting moment, they stood close, his hands still resting at her sides, their foggy breaths mingling in the chilly air between them.

Something shifted in his eyes, a flicker of the same heated connection they'd shared in the shed.

Her heart stuttered.

He released her and stepped back, clearing his throat. "Best get you inside before you freeze."

She nodded, the bite of cold surging once more.

As Miles led the horses to the barn, she gathered her skirts and crunched through the snow to the front door.

Before she could reach for the latch, the door swung open, revealing Dinah's relieved face. "Clara! Thank the Lord. We were about to send some of the men out searching for you two."

"I'm so sorry we worried you." Her face was too numb to smile as she stepped into the welcoming heat of the house. "The storm came on so quickly. We had to take shelter in a shed until the wind let up."

Surprise flashed in Dinah's eyes, twisting a knot in Clara's chest.

Maybe she shouldn't have mentioned the shed. Miles probably wanted to tell his family about her knowledge in a quiet way. Would Dinah guess they'd taken refuge in the outbuilding where the sapphires were stored? Miles had said they had other buildings in some of the pastures for hay and tools.

But before she could find a way to set the woman's mind at ease, a familiar voice cut through the room. "Miss Pendleton. I've been waiting for you."

Panic knotted her stomach as she peered around Dinah to see Emmett Holloway rising from his seat at the dining table.

Uncle Hiram sat across from him, his weathered face unreadable.

She fought to keep her own expression neutral. She had to stay calm and polite, not let her roiling emotions betray her. Showing weakness could ruin everything.

"Mr. Holloway." She dipped her chin in a respectful nod. "I apologize for my absence. The storm caught us unawares."

His sharp eyes studied her, as if trying to pluck secrets from her skin. " It seems you've had quite the adventure." He glanced briefly at Uncle Hiram before rising to his feet.

Her uncle stood as well, his lined face creased with concern. "Clara, are you all right? You must be chilled to the bone." He moved to her side, reaching out to brush snow from her shoulders with his good hand.

She managed a tight smile. "I'm fine. Just a bit cold and tired." She avoided looking at Holloway. Just the sight of the man sent anger through her veins. How dare he try to steal from these wonderful people? Even if it was an order from a superior.

Holloway cleared his throat. "Well, I'm glad you made it back safely. The weather can be treacherous this time of year." His tone was pleasant enough, but his voice hinted at suspicion.

Or maybe that was her imagination. *Lord, show me how to best him.*

He straightened. "I need to head back, but I brought notes for you. I left them in my saddle bag, so please walk with me to the barn."

She summoned a smile, doing her best to keep it from wavering. "Of course."

Holloway strode to the door, holding it open for her. She stepped out into the biting cold once more, her breath misting in the air.

They crunched through the snow in silence. Her heart pounded against her ribs. She had to find the right words, the best way to handle this.

Just before they reached the barn, the door opened, and Miles stepped out. He appeared surprised to see Holloway—and her with the man—but when Holloway dipped his chin in greeting, Miles returned the gesture.

Then his gaze met Clara's, searching. She wanted desperately to give him a sign, to beg him for help in getting rid of this threat. But she didn't dare.

Instead, she forced a pleasant expression. "Mr. Holloway came to deliver their survey notes."

"Mrs. Coulter gave me the food already," Holloway said. "It's packed in my bags."

The food. A new churning started in her middle. She'd not given it a single thought since leaving in the sleigh with Miles. At least she'd finished cooking before they headed out.

"Would you like help with your horse?" Miles's words were

for Holloway, but his gaze held her, asking the same question. *Do you need help?*

She had no choice but to shake her head. She would be all right. She just had to satisfy Holloway's questions enough to get rid of the man.

"He's all saddled and ready. I need to speak with Miss Pendleton alone. It'll only take a minute." Holloway held the barn door open for her, clearly waiting for Miles to move on.

With a final look at her, Miles finally walked on toward the house.

As the barn door closed behind her, desperation wove through her chest. In the dim space, the rich scent of hay and horses enveloped her but did nothing to calm her nerves.

Holloway led her to where his horse was tethered. He made a show of rifling through his saddlebags, then pulled out a wad of papers. Finally, he turned to face her, thrusting them out, his expression hard. "Well, Miss Pendleton? I trust you've made progress on our project."

She fought the urge to shrink back from his penetrating stare, taking the notes instead. "I'm afraid not. There's been no opportunity to resume the search."

His brows lowered. "You've had several days now. You should have made opportunities to get at the other places. Created distractions."

Her chest clenched so tight, it was hard to breathe. "It's not that simple. The families from two other houses have been staying here. The men keep themselves armed, and they've even been posting a guard. With the cold weather keeping everyone else inside, there's been no chance."

"I thought you were clever enough to manage it." His tone sharpened with impatience. "I guess I'll have to create the distraction for you."

Panic flared through her. "Like what? What would you do?"

His gaze narrowed on her. "Leave that to me. But when it

CHAPTER 14

The next day, Miles stood near the crackling fire, the warmth from the flames doing little to chase away the chill of unease that had settled over him with this conversation. His brothers and Eric sat or stood in the chairs around the hearth, their faces grim as they discussed their next steps.

The close quarters of the cabin and bunkhouse were wearing on everyone, and they needed to find and eliminate the threat so Eric's and Jude's families could return safely to their own homes.

And so the work on Jonah's cabin could continue. No one could miss how eager Jonah and Patsy were for their home to be finished so their wedding could take place. They'd hoped for a Christmas ceremony. Since that holiday was just over a week away, it would likely be closer to New Year's before they could be married and move into their new home.

Miles couldn't help a glance over at the kitchen, where Clara worked with Patsy and Jess, cooking for the survey camp and all the hungry bellies here.

"Do we think it's a stranger trying to steal from us? Or

someone from Mick's operation?" Jude leaned forward, arms braced on his knees.

Jonah frowned. "If anyone's out there now, we should find their tracks in the snow."

"We need to search the area again." Jericho's tone held its usual decisiveness. "Two men stay here to protect the house. The rest of us will ride out and scour every inch of this land until we find whoever is behind this."

A sound plan. Gil would likely want to stay here with Jess, and—

The front door opened, letting in a gust of cold air ahead of Naomi. She'd been working in the bunkhouse. She closed the door and scanned the room.

Their conversation paused at the worry in Naomi's expression. Her gaze landed on her husband, Eric. "Have you seen Anna?" She flicked a look at the rest of them. "I was putting Mary Ellen down for a nap and sent Anna here to fetch a basket of sewing a quarter hour ago. She hasn't returned."

Eric rose. "She hasn't come in here." He looked around the room. "Right?"

"I haven't seen her." A knot of worry tightened in Miles's gut as the other men also confirmed they hadn't seen the little girl. The bunkhouse was only steps away from this cabin. Where could she have gone?

Naomi's brow furrowed. "She should have been back at least ten minutes ago." Her voice rose with worry.

In an instant, everyone was on their feet, all the women coming from the cookstove except Clara, who stirred the contents of a pot, but watched the group with concern in her gaze.

"We'll find her." Eric wrapped an arm around his wife. "She can't have gone far."

Once outside, they all fanned in different directions. Miles headed for the barn at a run. They'd trekked this route so much, the trail had been trod down much more than anywhere else.

He pushed open the heavy barn door. "Anna? Are you in here?" His voice echoed in the quiet space, but no cheerful, childish voice called back.

Sean followed him in, and they checked every stall, then the hayloft.

No sign of her.

Dread twisted tighter as he and Sean left the barn, looked in the corrals, then crossed to the bunkhouse. Eric and Naomi had just come out of the door.

Naomi's eyes rimmed rid, and Eric's hair had splayed from the frantic raking of his fingers.

"Any sign of her?" Eric's voice sounded strained.

"Nothing in the barn or corrals." He glanced around the edges of the clearing, where the others were searching. "You checked the bunkhouse?"

"She's not there." Naomi's words choked. "Only Mary Ellen, who's still sleeping."

Eric frowned as he stared into the distance. "We know she left the bunkhouse and never made it to the cabin. I already looked in the outhouse." He glanced at the ground around them. "Too bad there's so many tracks here."

As Eric spoke the words, something odd snagged Miles's gaze. Footprints. Toward the side of the bunkhouse.

He stepped closer to better see the tracks. They were blurred, like someone had dragged their feet.

Eric crouched beside him. "Whose are these?"

Miles pointed "They look like a man's boots, and the toes dug deep into the snow. Like he was carrying something heavy." He looked over at Eric and Naomi, who'd lowered beside her husband. "Do you know who might have walked from the woods to the door, then back to the trees?"

"Are you sure he started from the forest?" She glanced at

Eric. "One of the men might have gone out there this morning." To relieve themselves, no doubt. An easier trek than all the way up to the outhouse beyond the main cabin.

Miles turned back to the prints to make sure he'd seen right. "Look how the trail back to the woods lands on top of the first prints to the bunkhouse door."

The weight of the discovery pressed hard on his chest. Was it possible?

Eric surged to his feet and bolted toward the trees.

"Wait. Eric." Miles caught his arm. "We need to tell Jericho." If the stranger lurking around had taken Anna, they needed to be careful how they went after her.

But Eric shrugged away and disappeared into the shadow of the woods.

Miles whirled back to Naomi and motioned up the hill where the others were searching. "Go tell Jericho. Quick."

She scrambled that direction, and Miles followed Eric. He couldn't let his friend go alone. Especially if the scoundrel they chased had kidnapped such an innocent young girl.

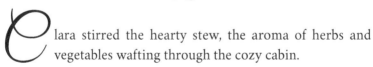

Clara stirred the hearty stew, the aroma of herbs and vegetables wafting through the cozy cabin.

The smells made her want to vomit.

Outside, frantic shouts echoed as the others searched for little Anna. Even Uncle Hiram had gone out to help. Her pretense for staying inside was that she couldn't leave the food. Not that anyone had stopped to ask.

Not when a seven-year-old girl was missing.

Could Anna really be lost?

This was the distraction Holloway had promised. Her chance to search Dinah and Jericho's room.

She'd expected another fire, maybe gunshots. Something

that would get the men running, the women stepping outside to see.

She hadn't expected this.

She set the wooden spoon aside with trembling hands. How could Holloway stoop to snatching an innocent child? Bile rose in her throat at the thought of Anna's cherubic smile, then those beautiful eyes wide as she faced whatever Holloway had done with her.

Protect her, Lord. Comfort her.

She'd hoped there was some shred of decency in the man, that she could reason with him. But using an innocent girl to manipulate Clara? It made her insides churn. Even if he returned the child unharmed, the terror she must be feeling out there alone in the wilderness...

Clara would have to play along, make him believe she was cooperating in his scheme to get the deed.

An idea occurred to her.

She could forge the deed, buy herself time and get Holloway to move on. But first, she needed to find the real document.

The front door was securely shut, the place empty except for her.

She slipped into Dinah and Jericho's empty bed chamber, pausing just long enough to take in the furniture. There were a few likely hiding spots—the dressing table, the two chests of drawers, and the trunk at the foot of the bed. After a glance at the door, she approached the dressing table first, with its delicate curves and intricate carvings. Tugging open the first drawer, she wondered... Had Miles's made this? It was a work of art, and from what she'd seen, he was more than capable.

A lump tightened her throat as she searched that drawer, then the next. Ribbons, hairpins, and small trinkets greeted her, but no deed.

She moved on to the first of the two chests of drawers standing side by side. The clothing in two of the drawers appeared to belong to Dinah, and the rest held linens and cloth. No paper at all.

The other chest held Jericho's clothes, and she moved as quickly as she could, listening for the crinkle of paper.

With each passing moment, the weight of her deception grew heavier on her shoulders. She was betraying the trust of the Coulters, the very people who'd done so much for her and Uncle Hiram. The people she'd come to care for deeply. Yet, the alternative—allowing Holloway to carry out his awful plan unchecked—was unthinkable.

The heavy trunk lid rose with a creak that echoed throughout the room. She rifled through quilts and other fabrics.

Then her fingers tapped wood. She lifted the cloth to see a small wooden box. Could this be it?

With shaking hands, she lifted it out and opened it, revealing a stack of papers of various sizes. She combed through them, her eyes scanning each one until the words at the top of a paper snagged her gaze. *Homestead Deed.*

Her heart thundered so fast that she could barely breathe.

She pulled the deed from the box, confirmed she'd read the title correctly, then replaced everything else. Did the quilts look undisturbed? As much as she could tell.

She closed the lid and scanned the room once more to make sure nothing was out of place, then hurried back to the main room.

All remained quiet here, save the crackling of the fire in the hearth, the quiet bubble of the stew in the pot on the cookstove, and the frantic shouts for Anna drifting in from outside.

She had to help in the search. Maybe if Holloway was watching from nearby, he would release Anna once he saw Clara come out of the house.

She slipped into the chamber she shared with Uncle Hiram and knelt beside her bag. Opening the folded paper, she studied the elegant scrawl that filled both sides of the page. She could copy this well enough. The style wasn't unusual. She'd have to find similar paper. High quality, with no hint of a manufacturer's mark pressed into it. Could she make new paper look aged like this? Maybe.

She'd have to try. Holloway wouldn't know the exact condition of this document, so it wouldn't have to be identical.

Was it possible to copy this deed exactly, but make a small change Holloway wouldn't notice, yet a claims office would? Perhaps she could change the spelling of the claims office. Or maybe the name of the register who'd signed the deed. Surely, she could find something that would work.

For now, she tucked the paper down under her folded skirts, then scurried back to the main room and the stove. She stirred the soup and moved the pot to a cooler surface. The aromas didn't make her quite as ill now. She had a plan. One that would keep both the Coulters *and* their property safe—and her uncle— if all went right.

She strode toward the door, grabbing her coat and gloves on her way out.

The crisp mountain air filled her lungs as she stepped onto the stoop. Shouts of Anna's name echoed through the clearing, each one more desperate than the last.

Most seemed to come from down the hill, in the trees past the barn and bunkhouse. That made sense, for Anna and her family had been staying in the bunkhouse. Holloway had likely snatched her nearby.

Anger burned hotter inside her. He couldn't win this battle, and she wouldn't let him hurt this family again just to teach her a lesson.

She hurried in that direction, going wide around the barn and corrals. Should she check the barn and bunkhouse once more? Just in case? Something in her chest nudged her toward them.

She veered left to the barn door, slipping inside. The dim light made it hard to see. And surely the others had searched here already. But she did a quick scan of each stall and climbed the ladder to the hayloft, just in case.

No one.

She plunged back into the cold wind and jogged around to the bunkhouse. The barn and bunkhouse shared a wall, and the door to the latter was positioned at the side.

She pushed open the door and stepped in, her cheeks relieved to be out of the wind once more. A fire crackled in the hearth, and as she scanned the beds, her gaze stumbled on a sleeping child.

Mary Ellen.

Not Anna.

The tiny moment of hope deflated. The two-year-old must be taking her morning nap, unaware of all the chaos among the people she loved.

Clara tiptoed along the rows of bunks, checking beneath each and on every mattress tick. Just in case. This room was dim, the cloudy day outside letting in little sunlight through the single window. And the fire at the other end of the room didn't add much brightness.

As she reached the last set of bunks, she nearly missed the wide blue eyes staring at her from the face of a terrified little girl.

CHAPTER 15

*C*lara's heart twisted at sight of the little girl wedged behind the last set of bunks, her knees drawn up to her chest, her sweet face streaked with tears. "Anna. Thank God."

The child's eyes widened, and she pressed a finger to her lips. "Shhhh," she breathed, her voice barely audible. "He might hear you."

Oh, Lord. Clara moved closer and knelt beside the bunk, reaching out a hand. "Anna, sweetheart, it's me. It's Clara. You're safe now. I promise."

Anna's lower lip quivered, but she didn't move from her hiding spot. "Is he gone?" Her voice was small, frightened.

"Who, darling? Who are you afraid of?" Though she already knew the answer.

"The scary man. The one who grabbed me." A tear slipped down her cheek. "He said if I made a sound, he'd hurt Mama and Papa."

Fury and guilt warred within Clara. Holloway had terrorized this innocent child, all to manipulate Clara. She swallowed hard, forcing her voice to remain calm and soothing. "He's gone now, Anna. He's not going to hurt you or anyone else. I promise."

She wouldn't allow it.

Clara needed to get her out of there. But she had to call the others too. She reached for Anna's hand. "Come on. Let's go tell your mama and papa you're safe. Everyone is so worried about you."

How had Holloway gotten Anna back into the bunkroom without anyone seeing? Maybe when Naomi came to the house to look for Anna? He was such a...she couldn't think of words awful enough to suit him. *Keep him away from here, Lord. Please. Don't let him hurt these people.*

Anna took her hand, and Clara helped her stand, then wrapped an arm around her frail shoulders as they walked to the door.

Once outside, Clara tucked the girl closer against the wind and shut the door so her shout wouldn't wake Mary Ellen. Better they not have two frightened children on their hands.

Drawing a deep breath, Clara called out, her voice carrying across the clearing. "I found her! Anna's here, she's safe."

The shouts ceased abruptly, replaced by the thunder of running footsteps. Within moments, Naomi burst around the corner of the bunkhouse, her face pale and stricken. "Anna? Oh, thank the Lord!"

She fell to her knees, gathering the little girl into her arms as fresh tears streamed down both their faces.

Eric was right behind her, enfolding his wife and their daughter in a fierce embrace. Even Patsy crowded close, rubbing Anna's back.

Clara stepped away, her own eyes stinging as she watched the reunion.

Uncle Hiram and the others soon joined them, their relief palpable.

"Where was she?" Naomi's voice trembled as she still held Anna close.

"In the bunkhouse, hiding behind the last set of bunks." Clara spoke softly. "She was terrified."

Eric's jaw tightened, a fierce glint in his eye. "Did she say what happened? Who took her?"

Clara hesitated, her gaze darting to Anna's tearstained face. She couldn't very well blurt out Holloway's name. "Perhaps we should get her inside first, let her warm up by the fire. I have stew on the stove."

Anna could tell what happened, and the family could decide what to do from there.

For her own part, she needed to be alone—very alone—to start copying the deed.

Naomi rose to her feet, Anna tucked against her side.

The group made their way back to the main house, a somber silence hanging over them.

As they entered the cabin, the savory aroma of the stew filled the air, but Clara had lost all appetite. She busied herself ladling out bowls for everyone, trying to ignore the weight of the deed hidden in her pocket.

Most of the group huddled around the large fireplace, the family snuggling their rescued daughter close. Eric had carried Mary Ellen up with them so they could all be here at the main house, and the tot still wore a sleepy, confused look as she took in the clamor.

Miles stepped away from the others, coming to stand near Clara at the stove. He didn't speak at first, which made the weight on her chest press even harder. She could barely breathe.

When he finally spoke, his voice came out low, gentle. "Are you all right?"

Clara forced a smile, trying to keep her voice steady, her eyes on the food. "I'm just glad she's safe. It was a miracle we found her."

He studied her for a moment. "You're sure? If there's anything I can do, just say the word."

Anything he could do about what? Surely, he didn't know about the mess with Holloway. He was simply worried about Anna, right?

She swallowed the rush of heat threatening her eyes. She couldn't cry.

"Clara?" The tenderness in Miles's voice nearly undid her.

She forced herself to meet his gaze, her heart aching at the concern in his warm brown eyes. She wanted nothing more than to confide in him, to lean on his strength and let him help shoulder this burden. But she couldn't risk putting her uncle in danger. Or Miles and his family in danger. This was her battle to fight, her mistake to fix.

She mustered a smile. "I'm sure, Miles. Thank you. I'm just… overwhelmed with relief that Anna is safe. And still a bit shaken by what could have happened."

He nodded slowly, a flicker of doubt lingering in his eyes. "I understand. I'm grateful you found her when you did. Who knows what that scoundrel might have done."

Her stomach clenched. The guilt was a leaden weight in her chest, smothering each breath.

As he walked away, she braced her hands on the edge of the cast iron stove, trying to draw strength from its solid warmth. *Lord, guide me. Show me how to make this right.*

∼

*M*iles studied Clara from across the room. She still lingered at the stove, scooping stew into bowls, then handing them to Dinah, who carried them to the table.

She took pleasure in feeding people, he'd realized that early on. But the lines gathered on her brow now showed no sign of

121

delight. Her golden-brown hair, usually so neatly pinned, escaped in wispy tendrils around her face.

He wanted to wrap his arms around her and pull her to his chest. Smooth back those stray locks and soothe the worry from her eyes. Recover the closeness they'd shared waiting out the storm in the storage shed.

What bothered her so?

Was it worry that the man who took Anna might come back and do worse? That was a concern that churned in his own belly. But something about her manner seemed...distracted. Had she experienced a similar event in her past? Could she relate to the fear Anna must have felt? Maybe she'd been drawn into her own awful memories.

"Outside, men. All of us." Jericho's voice cut through his thoughts.

He tore his gaze from Clara and followed his brothers out into the yard. The icy air stung his face, a stark contrast to the warmth of the cabin.

They gathered in a tight group, even Sean, though Jericho surely wouldn't let the boy help with the search they were about to head out on. At eight years old, the lad tagged along with his uncles every time he was allowed.

"Let's move forward with our plan from before." Jericho shot a look between Gil and Miles. "You two stay here and stay, on guard. One at the barn window and the other at the house window. That way you'll be able to see in all directions." He leveled a stern look at them both. "Keep watch with your rifle every minute. I'm relying on the two of you to protect our women and children."

Something in his tone made it sound like he might be second-guessing giving such an important task to them. Gil was fourth in line by age, so he carried a bit of respect in Jericho's eyes. But Miles was the youngest. He'd likely always be seen as the baby, especially by their eldest brother.

The only way to change Jericho's mind was to prove himself, every time.

He met his gaze head-on. "I'll take the barn. You can count on me."

Jericho searched his face for a long moment before giving a curt nod. "Good. Gil, you've got the house then."

"Got it." Gil gave a solid nod.

Jericho turned to the others. "The rest of you, pair up and head out in your assigned directions. Keep your eyes sharp and your guns ready."

As they dispersed, Sean made to follow them, but Jericho caught him by the shoulder. "I need you to stay here and help Gil in the house."

The boy's expression drooped, but he followed Gil inside.

Miles understood how he felt. He'd been on the outside while his big brothers handled the important things often enough in his life. Now that he was old enough to take part, a small part of him longed for the simpler days, when he could trust the adults to make everything all right.

Now, it was up to him to protect the ones he loved. His brothers, their families.

Clara.

He made his way to the barn while the others saddled their horses, and within minutes the only sounds around him were the crackle of fire in the heater and the munching of the milk cow eating hay in her stall.

He positioned himself with his rifle by the window nearest the door, sitting on the barrel Clara had used when she worked here on her maps. If only she could be with him now.

They could talk as they had before. Maybe she would tell him what troubled her. Perhaps he could even comfort her a bit.

But she was needed in the cabin, helping to keep everyone calm and cared for.

And if he was being honest with himself, having her here

might be more of a distraction. He had to focus on watching for any disturbance outside, to prove to Jericho he could handle this responsibility.

He swept the trees, his finger resting lightly on the trigger. He would keep watch for as long as it took to ensure the safety of those he cared about.

Especially Clara.

CHAPTER 16

$\mathcal{C}$lara slipped into the bedchamber she shared with Uncle Hiram, easing the door closed behind her. Sunlight streamed through the small window, casting a warm glow on the floor beside her small bed. She took a deep breath, gathering her courage. This was her chance to finally get a proper look at the deed.

She sat on the floor on the far side of her cot, her back to the door, and pulled her carpet bag close. If someone came in unexpectedly, she could quickly tuck the paper out of sight.

Her fingers trembled a little as she unfolded the deed.

Across the top, the word *Homestead* had been written in a bold hand. The remaining text appeared to be standard, granting 160 acres to J. M. Coulter according to the Homestead Act of 1862. The register at the land office of Helena, Montana had signed the document—Henry M. Atkinson.

Nothing seemed out of the ordinary, though she'd never seen a homestead grant. She'd only laid eyes on one other deed —that to Uncle Hiram's farm. He'd been working in his office one day when she wandered in, and he took the time to explain what he was doing. Uncle Hiram always made her feel important, even as a young girl.

She inhaled a breath. She was doing this to protect her uncle. And Miles. And all of Miles's family.

As she released the air, she pulled her map sketchbook from her bag and opened to a blank page at the back. She cut out a sheet the same size as the homestead grant and laid the clean paper atop the aged document.

The thickness was different—her map paper a better quality. Surely Holloway wouldn't notice the discrepancy. Had he even seen a homestead grant? He may have, which was why she had to stay as close as she could to the original format. She could change names, and hopefully that would alert the clerk if Holloway took this to a land office to be signed over to someone else.

She crouched over the papers, dipped her pen in her inkwell, and traced the deed onto the clean paper. She had to keep a steady flowing hand so the ink wouldn't pool or splotch. Instead of making the grant out to J. M. Coulter, she wrote T. B. Coulter. If Mr. Coulter's name were listed in a ledger book, surely that difference would leap out to the clerk, enough to make him pause and investigate further anyway.

At the end of the document, she changed the name of the register who had signed from Henry M. Atkinson to Harold V. Wiltkinson.

Lord, let this be enough. Let the clerk spot the forgery. And protect my uncle and the Coulters.

Would her changes work? Or would they only make Holloway angry? Or Winston. If Holloway's claim that Winston had commanded this theft was true, where would this forged document go? The knot in her middle twisted tighter, and her throat swelled enough to make breathing hard.

Please, God. Protect me. Protect us all.

The original deed had once been folded, its crease deeply

worn and its edges stained from years of handling. She creased her new version in the same place, opening and closing the paper until the line was just as deep. She gathered some stain from the wooden floor on her fingers, mixing it with a dab of ink to dirty the edges of the document. After a few minutes of effort, it looked suitably aged. Or so she hoped, anyway.

She held up her work to the light. Maybe it wasn't identical to the Coulters' original deed, but it looked authentic. It would have to suffice. Holloway would never see the two side by side. She tucked the forged version into her pocket, then hid the original near the bottom of her carpet bag. She would return it to the Coulters' trunk at her first opportunity. Though without Holloway kidnapping a child to create a diversion, she couldn't imagine when that would be.

With everything done, she pushed to her feet and returned her bag to its place. As soon as the men returned, she'd take the evening meal to the survey camp—along with her other delivery.

But until then, she could help with the children. Maybe reading them a book or playing ranch with the animals like little Mary Ellen enjoyed so much.

It was the least she could do. Maybe she could somehow assuage the guilt pressing like a bear on her chest.

~

*L*ate the next morning, Clara stood on a chair, draping a garland of rich green pine boughs over the frame of the door leading into her chamber. The fresh scent of the evergreen filled her senses, bringing the warmth of Christmases past to fill her spirit.

Decorating for this holiday was the one time of year she and Sarah could work together with pleasure. They both loved all the festive trimmings, especially since most could be crafted using branches and berry clusters picked for free in the countryside. Clara loved beauty as much as Sarah did, especially when it could be had without spending hard earned wages.

"That looks just lovely, Clara." Naomi smiled as she approached, her arms laden with holly, crimson berries peeking out from glossy green leaves. "You have a real knack for where to place things."

Clara allowed a grin. "Thank you. Christmastime is my favorite season." She took several sprigs of holly from Naomi and wove them into the pine boughs, the bright red berries adding pops of color against the green.

"I do hope you and your uncle will stay and celebrate with us."

Warmth slid through Clara. "We're grateful you've let us stay this long." Could they possibly remain here until Christmas? Celebrating with Miles would be...too wonderful to let herself think about.

She stepped down from the chair, smoothing her skirts as she surveyed her work. The cabin was beginning to look festive, with garlands and ribbons adorning the walls and doorways. The scent of baking spices wafted from the kitchen, where Dinah and Patsy were preparing Christmas cookies.

Dinah placed a tray of dough in the oven and closed the door, then wandered toward them. "You ladies have performed a miracle. It's beautiful."

Heat crept up Clara's neck, but she didn't acknowledge any credit in the outcome. Naomi, Lillian, and Jess had done just as much. Angela had worked with them earlier this morning, but she'd been especially exhausted from the child she carried, so she'd laid down to rest while Mary Ellen napped.

"We need to finish planning the Christmas menu." Dinah propped her hands at her waist. "Naomi and I always make fig pudding and gingerbread. Of course we'll have whatever meat the men bring in. What are some of your favorite Christmas dishes, girls?"

Patsy was the first to speak. "I can make mince pie. That's something we always enjoyed. I'll bet Anna remembers it."

"Oh, that's perfect." Naomi tied ribbon into bows as she answered, then turned to Jess, who was positioning garland on the mantle. "What about you, Jess?"

The woman always seemed shy when spoken to in a group, and this time was no different. She ducked her chin, murmuring, "My father always loved my roasted chestnuts. There's a knack to knowing just when to pull them from the flame."

Did the others catch that Jess hadn't given her own choice, but her father's?

Clara hadn't heard the woman's story, but Miles mentioned she'd only been here a few weeks. Did she miss her family? Why wasn't she with them for Christmas?

Naomi sent Jess a warm smile. "I've never roasted chestnuts, but I imagine it's challenging. What's a food that *you* love?" Her emphasis on *you* couldn't be missed.

Jess stared into the flames. But then she sent a sheepish look to Naomi. "I think my favorite is roasted apples, hung over a fire until cooked through, then cut open and spread with butter."

Clara's middle gave a leap at the memory of how wonderful roasted apples tasted. Especially on a cold day when she sat by a warm blaze.

The door opened, and Miles stepped inside. Something surged in her middle at the sight of him. He was so handsome. And so capable.

His focus landed on her as he stomped snow from his boots onto the rug, and the concern in his eyes made her insides churn. This wasn't a warm meeting of gazes from across the room.

"Holloway's riding into the yard." His tone sounded as grim as his expression.

Her chest clenched, and a cold knot tightened in her middle.

She laid the holly she'd been about to hang on the table and started forward. Why would Holloway be here now? Surely it couldn't be about the forged deed she'd slipped into the meal delivery last night. Miles had insisted on delivering the food alone because of the unknown danger still lurking on the property, but she'd managed to tuck the paper, wrapped in a leather pouch, into the bag with the cornbread.

When she reached the door, she grabbed her coat. She couldn't let Holloway come inside. Whatever he wanted to say, she'd make sure he left the property as quickly as possible.

Miles touched her arm, drawing her gaze to his face. Those warm eyes held worry. "I'll go out with you." Though he didn't phrase it as a question, his gaze asked permission.

She shook her head. "He probably just wants to give me survey notes." The lie burned her through.

He *could* have come for that purpose.

But he'd sent sketches and measurements back with Miles the night before. She doubted he had anything new to share with her already.

Miles's brows drew together, but he stepped away, allowing her space to exit the cabin. She glanced over her shoulder as she crunched through the snow. He'd closed the door, but he probably watched from the window.

Relief wrapped around her, giving her a layer of protection from whatever Holloway would thrust on her now.

The man had already dismounted and waited beside his horse for her approach. His weathered face wore its usual sullen frown, but his eyes gleamed. "Miss Pendleton. I came to retrieve you and your uncle. We're done measuring this area, and we need to move on."

Cold dread crept through her veins.

No.

She'd known this moment would come, but...she shouldn't

have allowed herself to hope they might stay through Christmas. She wanted more precious days with Miles. And his family.

"The Coulters have invited us to stay through Christmas. Surely, a few more days wouldn't hurt the survey work. We could have a short Christmas holiday."

Holloway's expression hardened, implacable as stone. "It's time to leave. Now. Go fetch your uncle and gather your things."

She could only stare at him as her mind whirled. She guessed the deed had been the only thing that had made him linger. That awful, horrible business.

Anger surged through her, but she could do nothing about it.

Locking her jaw, she gritted out, "Very well." She had to get away from this man before she did something she'd regret.

She turned back to the house so he couldn't see the tears burning in her eyes. Each step toward the cabin felt like a mile, her legs leaden with dread.

How could she tell Miles she was leaving? How could she say goodbye to this wonderful place, these people she'd come to love?

She pushed open the door, the cheerful warmth of the cabin a stark contrast to the icy cold gripping her heart.

Miles was there in an instant, his hands gentle as he pulled her inside and closed the door behind her. "What did he want?"

She fought hard against the tears burning her eyes. "He says…it's time for us to leave. Today. That we need to move on with the survey team."

"No!"

His shout had her heart clenching tighter.

His chest rose and fell, fast, as if he worked to collect himself. "Can't you…?" His voice came out quieter. "Can't you stay until Christmas at least? I'll talk to him. Invite the rest of the men."

Clara shook her head, a single tear escaping to trail down

her cheek. "I asked. He wouldn't yield. I...I need to tell my uncle."

She made to step around Miles, but he caught her arm, his grip gentle but firm. "Clara, wait. Please. There has to be something we can do. Some way to change his mind."

His earnestness, the desperate hope in his eyes, nearly undid her. She wanted so badly to find a solution. But what could they do?

Holloway held the authority, and she couldn't risk angering him and somehow exposing the forged deed.

"I don't know, Miles." Her voice cracked with the pain rending her heart. "I don't think so."

She couldn't stand here looking at him. Every second so close to him made her want to plunge herself into his arms. To beg him to hide her so she didn't have to leave.

She turned away. "I have to go." She hurried toward the chamber where her uncle was resting. Holloway wouldn't be kept waiting long.

When she opened the door, Uncle Hiram sat on the edge of the bed, his injured hand cradled in his lap. He'd recovered a great deal and seemed to have much of his strength back.

He looked up as she entered, a smile lighting his features until he caught sight of her expression.

"What's wrong, my dear?" He rose to meet her.

She closed the door and swallowed hard, trying to steady her voice. "Mr. Holloway is here. He says it's time for us to move on with the survey team. He's waiting for us now."

Uncle Hiram's brow furrowed, but he didn't speak for a moment. Surely, he wanted to stay as much as she did.

She stepped toward him, a tiny bit of hope building in her chest. "Do you think...do we really need to keep working with the surveyors? Couldn't we find work around here instead? Especially with your hand still injured."

She trailed off as he shook his head, his mouth forming a

grim line. "I wish we could, my girl. But we made a commitment to the survey team, and we need to see it through."

Her chest ached, her throat so tight she could barely breathe. Fresh tears welled in her eyes, blurring her vision.

Uncle Hiram rested a hand on her shoulder. "Maybe once our work is done, we can come back to this place. If you still have a hankering for it." His voice softened even more with those last words.

Clara nodded, swallowing past the lump in her throat. If she told him about the deed, that would surely change his mind.

Yet it would cause him so much pain. To know both about Holloway's demand and how she'd gone along with it. Maybe she should have confided in him to begin with.

She couldn't go back now though.

She'd made a plan, and any deviation from it could tip Holloway off that she'd double-crossed him.

As little as she wanted to leave, she needed Holloway a long way from the Coulters.

She swiped at her tears and drew in a steadying breath. "We'd best not keep him waiting."

Her uncle squeezed her shoulder. "You're a strong girl, Clara. We'll get through this. And like I said, maybe we can come back someday."

She nodded, not trusting her voice. Knowing that coming back wouldn't be an option, not if the Coulters ever found out what she'd done.

It seemed she had no choice, no matter how much leaving broke her heart.

CHAPTER 17

When Clara carried her belongings into the main room a few minutes later, Miles was waiting.

He stood by the hearth, his hands braced on the mantle, his head bowed. At the sound of their footsteps, he turned. Raw pain etched his features, twisting her heart.

She took a step toward him. Everything in her craved to feel his strength, his warmth, one last time. "Miles."

He met her halfway, his arms coming around her in a fierce embrace.

She sank against him, breathing in his scent of pine and wood smoke. If only she could stay here forever, sheltered in his arms.

Sounds drifted around them. Uncle Hiram speaking with the women, exchanging goodbyes. Her eyes burned, but she focused on the feeling of Miles.

Too soon, she forced herself to pull away. Enough to look at him, though she didn't leave his arms. Not yet.

Tears glimmered in his eyes, and the sight nearly undid her. That this strong man would think of her worthy of such emotion.

When he spoke, his voice came out low and rough. "I know you have to go, but..." He hesitated, searching her eyes. "Will you write to me? Let me know you're all right?"

She nodded. "I will."

His throat worked. "Send me your address when you'll be in one place a while."

She could only manage to say again, "I will."

He pressed a kiss to her forehead, his lips warm and soft against her skin. She let her eyes drift shut, taking in this last tenderness.

But then he released her, and she had to turn away. Cold rushed against her body without his touch.

She turned to her uncle, standing by the door with his carpetbag in his hand, his eyes filled with sympathy.

Dinah and Naomi lingered beside him, and she accepted a hug from them each. Dinah's whispered, "Come back to us when you can," nearly released the tears she was fighting to hold back.

But she bid goodbye to the rest and followed her uncle outside. The icy air built up her defenses. Maybe this goodbye would only be temporary.

Someday, maybe she could find her way back to Miles...and the unexpected home she'd found in his arms.

~

Clara's stomach churned as her mount followed Uncle Hiram's down the mountain trail. Holloway's horse nudged close behind her own. Pushing. Blocking her from even the thought of turning back.

She *would* return to him though. After they finished the surveying they'd signed on to do, she would find a way back to the Coulter ranch.

Back to Miles.

What if she couldn't? What if something happened with her uncle? What if they reached the west coast and he could no longer travel? He'd been so good to her. She couldn't abandon him if he needed her.

Or, what if she did manage to return, only to find out that the Coulters had discovered her part in the attempt to steal their land?

She'd tried to save it, to protect them. Would they see it that way? Or only see betrayal?

She couldn't worry about any of it. It was done, and she was leaving. She'd deal with tomorrow, tomorrow.

As she worked to shift her mind onto something else, a reminder slipped in, one that made her lungs cease working.

The deed.

She'd forgotten to put the Coulters' real deed back in the trunk.

She still carried it at the bottom of her carpet bag. Didn't she?

Yes.

Her middle knotted. She couldn't leave with it. She'd be worse than Holloway.

How could she get it back to them? Could she make an excuse that she'd forgotten something? Would Holloway let her ride back?

As hard as he was pushing her horse from behind, it didn't seem likely. Could she leave the paper in a safe place? Somewhere the Coulters would find it? Maybe they'd come down to the survey camp after they left to check the site. But she couldn't just leave such an important paper out in the open. And if it were hidden, they wouldn't find it.

Think, Clara. Think.

Another possibility occurred to her, and she examined the idea from all angles.

The shed where she and Miles had taken refuge from the

storm. Heat crept up her neck at the reminder of what had happened there. How it had changed their relationship.

Could it be the place to leave the deed? Maybe tucked between two crates? Surely, it would be safe among all those sapphires.

And if she weren't mistaken, the building was just a little farther down the trail. She'd glimpsed the back of it through the leafless trees while riding from the survey camp to the ranch house.

How could she get them to stop?

Maybe a female emergency? She couldn't think of anything that would be so urgent it couldn't wait until they reached the camp.

Maybe an issue with her gut? That might work.

She'd have to have the deed in her pocket already before she started drawing attention to her ailment. She nudged her horse to the right edge of the trail, so Holloway would be on the opposite side of her horse's rump as her bag.

Keeping her upper body at a natural angle, she eased her hand into the small opening left by the buckle, then fumbled around at the bottom of the bag until her fingers found paper. She grasped it tightly, pulled it out, then tucked it into the pocket of her skirt.

Now for the harder part.

They were almost to where she should be able to see the back of the shed through the trees. The moment she caught sight of it, she let out a low groan, clutching at her stomach.

"Uncle Hiram." She made her voice strained. "I'm not feeling well. I think I need to stop for a moment."

Her uncle reined in his horse, turning to look at her, concern etched on his weathered face. "What's the matter?"

"My stomach." She grimaced for effect. "The food I ate isn't settling. I need to find a privy. Urgently."

Holloway pulled up beside her, frowning. "Can't it wait till the camp?"

Clara shook her head, mustering a frantic expression. "It's urgent."

With a sigh, Holloway nodded. "Make it quick."

She slid from her saddle and handed her reins to her uncle and hurried into the trees, still gripping her middle.

She aimed toward the shed. Hopefully, Holloway wouldn't watch too closely. The building was nearly hidden unless one looked hard enough to see the structure through the branches.

Moving as quickly and quietly as possible, she slipped around to the door, pulled the latch, and pushed inside. The faint scent of charcoal blended with a damp odor, and the memory of the time they spent there was as vivid as the scene in front of her. Miles had sat right there, with her on his right, tucked against his side.

She shook herself, slipping the deed between two crates, leaving a little piece protruding so they'd be more likely to see it.

Don't let anyone else stumble across this, Lord. Help them to find it. Soon.

With the deed done, she spun and exited the building, pulling the door shut. She secured the latch.

Holloway's impatience had turned to a fierce expression by the time she returned to the horses.

She mounted her animal, avoiding the man's piercing gaze. Her uncle watched her with concern, but she managed a weak smile. "I'm feeling better now. Thank you for waiting."

Holloway grunted, kicking his horse. "Let's move. We've wasted enough time."

As they rode on, the knot in her middle loosened a little. Even so, she feared the Coulters would never find the deed.

Or what if someone else stumbled on it first?

No. The cabin was hidden for a reason. All these years, the

sapphires had stayed hidden. No reason to believe anyone would find it now.

Lord, guide them to that crucial piece of paper. Protect it. Protect them.

The sun had passed the noon mark by the time they reached camp.

Holloway dismounted, barking orders at the others to start packing. He turned to Clara, his expression hard. "Miss Pendleton, I need you to come with me. We have paperwork to attend to."

Her heart surged, and the knot in her middle tightened once more. "Paperwork?" What more could he need of her? Something in his tone told her this involved more than drawing maps.

He led her to the board they'd laid across a stump to use as a desk. "Sit." He motioned to the smaller log beside it.

She obeyed, and he laid several papers on the flat surface in front of her. The homestead deed she'd forged glared up at her, churning the bile in her stomach so much she might actually be sick. There were two other papers beside it. One glance told her what he planned.

He tapped on one. "Here's an example bill of sale. I want you to copy it on this blank paper." He tapped the other, as if his words hadn't been clear. "Use the same style of letters. Put in Coulter's name as the seller and the property description from the deed. Write the buyer's name as Marcus Winston. It needs to be perfect."

She couldn't breathe. Couldn't speak.

Not this madness again.

What was Holloway doing to her?

She should have anticipated this. She hadn't allowed herself to think much past the forging of the deed.

She'd been naive to ever think there could be a different endgame than the one she stared at now.

This step must prove that his orders were, indeed, coming from Winston. Why would Holloway carry out such an awful plan?

He must be getting a considerable cut.

He stood over her, his presence like a storm cloud. Or maybe a grizzly bear rearing on its hind legs. Daring her to defy him.

Did she dare?

On the other side of the camp, Uncle Hiram packed away the buckets and cooking supplies.

She could call to him, let him know what was happening.

But what could he do? If the other men were in on this deceit, it would be four against two. Even if they weren't, they'd take the side of their leader.

Holloway's voice sounded again, low and hard. "Let me remind you how awful it would be if your uncle were injured. Maybe his other hand scalded with boiling water to match the first. I'm sure you remember how awful his pain was."

Would he really do such a horrid thing?

Foolish question. He'd snatched and terrified a child. Of course he wouldn't hesitate to harm her uncle.

Her hand trembled as she picked up the pen. She'd come this far to keep him safe. She wasn't about to risk his wellbeing now.

She began to copy the bill of sale, keeping her script flowing across the page despite the turmoil within.

As she wrote, a small measure of relief settled through her. At least she had changed Mr. Coulter's initials on the forged deed. This document, as official as it might look, would not line up with the true deed. Perhaps that would be enough to cast doubt on the validity of the sale, should it ever come to light.

It was a small victory, but she clung to it as the only shred of hope she had left. She could only pray that, when the truth did come to light, the Coulters would understand the impossible choice she had faced.

As she finished the last flourish, she allowed herself a deep breath.

Holloway snatched the document from in front of her. "Good. Now, we have one other matter to attend to." He folded the bill of sale and tucked it into his coat pocket.

Her heart sank.

What more could he possibly want from her? She glanced around the camp.

The other men had nearly finished packing. Her uncle caught her eye, his brow furrowed with concern, but he was too far away to hear their conversation.

Holloway pulled her to her feet. "I need you to come sit over here." He half-dragged her to a pine tree, then pushed her to sit on the ground. Hard. Fear surged through her. What was he doing? He'd never man-handled her. Never even touched her.

"Hey!" Uncle Hiram's shout grabbed her attention, and she turned to see him being hauled by Tillman and Whitaker. He struggled against them, but with a man on either side, they were too strong.

"What are you doing?" She tried to keep her voice steady despite the fear coursing through her. "My uncle's done nothing."

Holloway ignored her as he picked up a length of rope. "Lean forward and put your hands behind you."

Panic sent her pulse racing.

His face was an impassive mask.

"What are you doing? Why are you tying us up?" She tried to scramble to her feet, but he shoved her back down.

"Don't make this harder than it has to be." His voice was cold, devoid of any hint of mercy. "You and your uncle are loose ends. Winston can't have you running your mouths about what you've done here."

Across the camp, Uncle Hiram's voice rose. "What's the

meaning of this?" He struggled against Tillman's and Whitaker's holds.

Tillman reared back and sent a fist into her uncle's gut.

He doubled over, his shoulders heaving.

Tears blurred her eyes. This couldn't be happening. She'd done everything Holloway asked. That should have kept them safe.

He pushed her shoulders forward, and she placed her hands behind her back as he'd asked. Rough rope bit into her wrists as he bound them. She couldn't see her uncle well from this position, only that his hair was askew as he still struggled against Tillman and Whitaker, though they were tying him to a tree now. Was that blood on his jaw?

Desperation welled inside her. "Let my uncle go. He doesn't know anything. I've not told him about the deed."

A mirthless bark escaped Holloway's lips as he pushed her back against the tree. "Right. And he'll just sit by and leave you here. Winston wants you both eliminated."

"Eliminated?" The word scorched like hot ash on her tongue. Surely, he couldn't mean...

Holloway grabbed another length of rope and wrapped it around her middle, pinning her arms to her sides and lashing her to the solid trunk. "Don't worry, I'm no murderer. I'll let nature take its course. Hunger, exposure, wild animals—one of them will get you eventually."

Clara's breath came in short, panicked gasps as the reality of their situation sank in.

Holloway was going to leave them here, tied to these trees to die slow, agonizing deaths.

And there was nothing she could do to stop it.

She twisted her wrists, testing the ropes.

They held fast. Holloway knew his knots.

Across the camp, Uncle Hiram had gone still, his chin

lowered. Blood dripped from his nose and the corner of his mouth. They'd beaten him into submission.

She had to try again. "Please. You don't have to do this. We won't tell anyone, I swear it."

He ignored her, just grabbed a length of chain and wound it around her. The heavy links pressed into her chest and made it hard to breathe. The cold metal seeped through her clothes, chilling her all the way through. When he finished, the chains held so tightly she could only move her head and legs.

Holloway stepped back to study his handiwork. Then he pulled a rag from his pocket.

No! She clamped her lips shut, but his grimy fingers pinched her nose until she had to gasp for air. After shoving the cloth between her teeth, he tied it behind her head, cutting off her cries. The taste of dirt and something else far worse filled her mouth.

Tears streamed down her face as he left her to secure Uncle Hiram in the same manner, tying a gag around his mouth a dozen yards away. Her uncle's eyes met hers, the sorrow so deep her heart wrenched in two.

CHAPTER 18

*H*olloway and the others mounted their horses, taking her mare and her uncle's gelding with them. None of the men even sent them a backward glance as they rode away. The sound of hoofbeats faded, replaced by an oppressive silence broken only by the rustling of leaves in the icy wind.

Panic rose like nausea, but she fought it back. She had to stay calm, had to think. There must be a way out of this. Her teeth had already begun to chatter. The chains were too tight to allow her body to tremble.

The flow leaking from her eyes absorbed into the nasty cloth over her face.

Across the camp, Uncle Hiram caught her gaze. She'd never seen him look so broken, so utterly hopeless.

This was all her fault. If she'd only spoken up, told Miles everything.

What a fool she'd been, trying to protect everyone, thinking she could handle this on her own.

She was no smarter, no more capable than that foolish seven-year-old girl who'd hastened her mother's death.

But she couldn't let despair overwhelm her. She had to *do* something. Her legs were helpless. She could only kick at the leaves and pine needles around her. The chains were too tight to allow her to shimmy up the tree and stand. What good would that do anyway?

If she could get the gag out of her mouth, she could call for help. They might even be close enough to the ranch house to be heard. Like that night she and Miles had heard Goodwin's violin. Or maybe Miles and his brothers would be out searching for the kidnapper.

She believed now the fire, the stranger creeping toward the house, even the dead cow. Holloway and the others had been responsible for all of it. Maybe he was trying to scare the Coulters, or just keep them off-kilter.

She wouldn't put anything past those men anymore.

She closed her eyes, and realization mixed with shame. Not once had she cried out for God's help since she and her uncle reached the camp with Holloway.

Lord, I'm sorry for not turning to You first. We need You. More than I've ever needed you before. Don't let my uncle die. Bring someone to save us. Show me what to do.

Letting herself rest in that prayer, she drew in a slow breath, as much as the chains would allow. Then released it just as slowly. *Thank you.* God never failed to share His peace when she asked.

She finally opened her eyes and set to work on the gag. Over and over, she rubbed her cheek against her shoulder, working to pull the fabric down from her mouth. He'd tied it so tightly though.

Minutes stretched into an eternity as she worked, her jaw aching, her neck burning from the strain. The knot wouldn't loosen.

She couldn't give up. Not now. Not ever.

Her face grew numb from the cold and the constant pressure. Her hands had long ago lost their feeling. Her legs too, now that she thought about it.

This wasn't working.

This wasn't working, and even if it did... What? What did she think was going to happen?

Nothing. Nothing was going to happen.

They were trapped. The sun was going down. And they were going to die.

And it was all her fault.

She gave up, working her jaw to release the ache.

As her teeth brushed the fabric, a new thought rose up. Maybe she could bite through the foul cloth.

Maybe if she did, then maybe...maybe someone would hear her call.

Anyway, she wouldn't quit until she breathed her last.

She clamped her teeth down on the rag, ignoring the acrid taste that filled her mouth. She worked at it, gnawing and pulling, her jaw screaming with the effort. The fabric was thick and unyielding.

At first.

Little by little, she worked her side teeth through the edge seam, until finally she heard a rip.

Now came more twisting and craning her neck as she used her shoulder to pull at the cloth, tearing the rip more and more. The tension in her gag eased. Not much, but enough to show she was making progress.

Help me get this, Lord.

Dusk had settled. How long had she sat here tugging at her gag? She could almost taste freedom though.

If freedom tasted like Holloway's filthy stocking.

She allowed her neck to rest a moment, then started again.

A blessed ripping sound surged hope through her.

Heart pounding, she redoubled her efforts, chomping on the weak spot. *Please, Lord, let this work. Let me save my uncle.*

With a final, desperate tug, the gag tore free, falling away from her face. She gulped in lungsful of frigid air, coughing and sputtering. Her throat was raw, her tongue thick and clumsy, but she'd done it.

She could call for help.

It was dark now, and she couldn't see her uncle. "Uncle Hiram! Are you all right?" The temperature had dropped with the sun, and her breath puffed in a cloud.

A muffled grunt was her only response. He must be still gagged. But at least he was alert. How badly had he been hurt?

Fresh strength surged through her. "Keep praying. I'm going to call for help."

She tried for a deep breath to yell, but the chains didn't give a bit. She used what breath she could and screamed, "Help!" Her voice came weak, no louder than the bleat of a goat.

She cleared her throat and tried again. "Help!" This time the word sounded stronger.

Pausing, she strained for any hint that she'd been heard.

Only the rustling of leaves on the breeze and the distant cry of a bird answered.

"Help!" She could try to yell something else, but it seemed that one word would get through better than a full sentence.

She continued to call, pausing every few tries to listen for a response. As the minutes ticked by with no answer, icy tendrils of fear crept up her spine.

What if no one was close enough to hear?

Taking in another shallow breath, she screamed as loud as her body could manage. "Help! Someone help!" Her voice broke on the last word.

It would weaken soon. Her entire body would weaken.

She strained to hear any return noise.

The mournful howl of a wolf carried on the icy wind.

God, no! Surely this wasn't the way the Lord planned for their lives to end.

I'm sorry, Father. I'm so sorry I participated in Holloway's sins. Please. Send someone to save us.

Clara let her head fall back against the rough bark of the tree, tears freezing on her cheeks. Their fate lay in God's hands alone. She had to trust that the Lord had a plan in this nightmare.

~

*I*n the barn, Miles scraped his knife over the wood in a steady motion, deepening the groove in the design he'd decided to carve into the rifle stock.

This would be a Christmas gift for Jericho, if Miles could finish it in time. But keeping his hands busy only allowed his mind to spin in circles.

Why had he let Clara go? *Lord, should I have asked her to stay?*

He'd been so blindsided by her sudden departure, his first reaction had been to assume God was taking her away.

That this was His way of saying she wasn't the one for him.

Yet, the connection with her had been so natural. She'd felt like an extension of himself, so easy to be with. Her heart as lovely as her face.

Had God been pushing him to take action? To share how he felt about her, and maybe ask her to stay?

Maybe she'd just needed to know how he felt. Needed to know she could have a future here.

They were both young. If she'd stay, they could take time to get to know each other better. But the thought of never seeing her again twisted a knot so tight in his insides that he could hardly breathe.

Should he go after her?

Darkness had fallen outside, bringing with it icy cold. The thought of her out there, in this weather...

He could be at their camp first thing in the morning and

follow their tracks. He would move faster than the group, and they would stop eventually to set up camp.

He would find them. Maybe she and her uncle would both agree to come back. But he couldn't let her go without trying. Without telling her how he felt. The alternative—a lifetime of wondering what might have been—was too painful to consider.

He needed to talk this through with someone. If only Sampson were here.

Maybe Jude, who possessed a thoughtful, steady wisdom that would help Miles see the situation from all angles.

Laying the knife and rifle on the workbench, he strode out of the barn and headed for the bunkhouse to find Jude and Angela. But as he neared the door, a sound made him pause.

It might have just been the wind, but he waited, listening hard. There it was again—a voice, faint. Almost like…

"Help!" The word came clearer this time.

His blood ran cold. Either he'd gone mad from losing Clara and his mind was summoning the sound of her voice.

Or she was in trouble.

He sprinted through the snow to the bunkhouse and burst in.

Everyone in the building looked up—both Jude's and Eric's families.

"Hurry!" He motioned for them to come outside. "Someone's calling for help. Come out and listen."

They all follow him into the frigid night, Eric carrying Mary Ellen and Naomi gripping Anna's hand.

The group stood silently, straining to hear over the howling wind. A beat passed, then another.

There. The sound came again, distant but unmistakable. "Help! Someone, please!"

His lungs squeezed out his breath. "It's Clara. I know it is." He spun toward the barn. "I'm going out to find her."

"Not alone you aren't." Jude's steady voice cut through the wind. "I'm coming with you. Eric, let the others know."

Within minutes, Miles and Jude were tightening girths when Jericho and Dinah pushed into the barn, followed by the rest of his family.

"We need to think this through." Jericho glanced between Miles and Jude. "What if it's a trap? Someone trying to lure us away from the house."

A cold fist squeezed Miles's lungs. He hadn't considered that. But the thought of Clara, alone and in danger, overrode all else. "It's a risk I have to take. That's Clara out there. I'll never forgive myself if something happens to her."

Jude shifted uneasily. "Miles is right. If it's Clara, we can't just leave her."

Jericho's lips pressed into a thin line, then he gave a curt nod. "All right. But I'm coming too. Jonah, stay here with Eric and Gil to guard the house and women."

"Should I ride with you?" Dinah looked up at her husband, worry furrowing her brow.

Jericho rested a hand on her shoulder, his eyes softening. "Stay here where you're safe. I can't risk you. If she's hurt, we'll bring her straight back."

Dinah's eyes glistened, but she nodded. "Go. Save her."

While Jericho readied his gelding, Miles and Jude tied blankets and a bit of food and water behind their saddles. They could each carry lanterns.

At last, they headed out the barn door. Angela stood next to Dinah as they passed. "We'll be praying for you."

"It sounds like she might be at their camp still." Miles called to his brothers as he turned that direction.

"Let's try it." Jericho nudged his mount beside Miles's, and they pushed the animals into a run.

CHAPTER 19

The horses had to drop down to a trot when they entered the woods.

The darkness pressed in around them as they shifted to single file, winding around branches and boulders almost covered by snow. Despite the shelter of the trees, icy wind still whipped against him. *Please, God. Let her be all right.*

Every few minutes, one of Clara's cries rose over the crunch of their horses' hooves in the snow—and the pounding of his heart. Her voice had grown raspy as if she'd been calling for hours.

Maybe she had been.

He cupped his hands around his mouth. "Clara! We're coming!"

Lord, please. Keep her safe until we can get to her.

He didn't stop to wait for her reply, but after a beat, her distant voice rasped, "Miles?"

The desperation in her voice spurred him on, and he urged his horse faster despite the treacherous terrain. His brothers kept pace behind him. The cries had to be coming from the survey camp. What could have happened there? A bear?

He gripped his rifle tighter as worst case scenarios flashed through his mind. Images of her injured and bloody. Unable to move.

The survey camp came into view across the creek. He called out again. "Clara! Are you hurt? Keep talking so we can find you."

Her reply was weak but close. "We're here! Uncle Hiram is hurt. Please, hurry!"

At last, they broke through the trees into the clearing where the survey camp had been set up. He pulled his horse to a halt, his brothers coming up short behind him.

"Clara!" The place looked empty in the darkness. Deserted.

"Here." Her voice drew him to the trees. A figure huddled at the base of one of the trunks.

He sprinted to her, rifle in hand. He should have grabbed the lantern from his saddle.

Why wasn't she moving?

He dropped to his knees beside her, but his mind scrambled to make sense of the metal wrapped around her. Chains? "What happened?"

He had to get her untied. But where was the end?

Jericho appeared at his side, lantern in hand.

Finally, Miles could see better. He followed the chains until he found an end tucked under one of the loops. He and his brother worked quickly to unwind the metal from around her. "Who did this to you? Where are the others?"

"Holloway." Her raspy voice trembled. "They tied us up and left us."

Fury surged through him. "Why would he do that?"

The last of the chain fell away, revealing rope also binding her to the tree. The man had taken pains to keep her locked tight.

To keep her here, vulnerable. Where she would've frozen to death by morning.

He couldn't think about that. Not yet.

Jericho sliced through the cord with his hunting knife, allowing Miles to focus on Clara.

The terror in her face twisted his insides. "Why did he do this?" He reached to cup one of her dirt smeared cheeks.

"I'll tell you in a minute." Worry lined her eyes. "My uncle. He's tied too, and he's hurt."

"Jude is freeing him." Jericho said as he released the last cord holding Clara to the tree.

She slumped forward, and Miles gripped her upper arms.

"Let me cut the rope at her wrists." Jericho's voice halted Miles from pulling her close, but he was ready.

As soon as her arms fell free, Miles pulled her against him, holding her tight. Her shivers vibrated through him, and he rubbed a hand up and down her back, trying to warm her. "You're safe now." He murmured the words into her hair. "I've got you."

She shuddered, and he pulled her closer, shifting from his knees to sit so he could bring her onto his lap. Her shaking hadn't lessened, and she clung to his jacket, as though she thought he might leave.

She needed a warm fire.

He needed to get her home.

Jericho stood. "I'll get blankets."

Miles wrapped as much of himself around her as he could, rocking to soothe her. *God, what happened here?*

So much turmoil churned inside him. Anger, fear. He couldn't sort through it all. The only thing he could do was hold Clara. Having her in his arms, being here with her, eased a bit of his panic. But he couldn't rest until he knew what happened. Knew she was truly all right.

She sniffed, her icy brow pushing against his neck. "I was so afraid," she whispered, her voice muffled. "I didn't know if anyone would find us."

"I'm so sorry I let you leave." He pressed a kiss to her hair, breathing in her sweet scent. "I should have asked you to stay. I wanted you to stay."

Jericho returned with blankets and draped them around Clara's shaking form. Miles tucked them closer, cocooning her against his chest.

"We're getting Hiram warm too." Jericho crouched in front of Clara. "Are you hurt?"

"No. Is my uncle?" Her voice was so small, and she felt impossibly fragile in his arms.

Jericho lifted his gaze toward where Jude must be helping the older man. "Looks like just a scrape on his face. I can't tell if the cold's caused damage or not." He refocused on Clara. "We need to get you both back to the house. Think you can ride?"

"Yes."

"Good." Jericho stood. "I'll bring Miles's horse over."

Within a few minutes, they had all loaded on the animals. Miles kept Clara seated in his lap, sideways in the saddle. They'd bundled a blanket around her head and shoulders, and another around her legs.

Father, don't let her or her uncle be permanently injured.

They kept a steady pace up the slope, the horses as eager as the rest of them to get home.

At last, they entered the clearing where the welcoming glow of lantern light spilled out from the cabin's windows. The others must have seen them coming, for his family spilled from the front door to meet them.

Dinah took charge immediately. "Bring them inside. Quickly."

Jonah reached up to take Clara from Miles. Part of him hated to let her go, but he forced himself to ease her into his brother's arms. Then he slid to the ground behind them.

"I'll take the horses." Eric reached for Miles's reins.

Miles trudged behind Jonah, and the others filed in with

them. Without Clara's warmth, the icy wind whipped through his coat and trousers.

How cold must she have been, on the ground, exposed to this?

The warmth of the cabin wrapped around him as he stepped inside, chasing away the cold that had seeped into his bones. It didn't lessen the cold fury surging through him toward the men who'd nearly killed Clara and her uncle.

Dinah directed Jonah to settle Clara on the armchair near the hearth, where a fire crackled.

Gil followed close behind, half-carrying an exhausted Hiram.

Miles sank onto the edge of the two-seat rocker adjacent to where Clara sat, leaving enough room for Dinah to work as she knelt before her.

"Are you hurt?" Dinah reached for the end of the blanket wrapped around Clara's arms.

She shook her head. "Just c-cold."

Dinah scanned Clara's upper body, then pulled the blanket tight again and shifted her focus to the lower covering. "I need to look at your feet."

As she pulled the blanket up to reveal Clara's boots, she called over her shoulder. "Na, I need that warm water."

Naomi appeared a second later with a pan of liquid.

Angela approached from the other side with a steaming mug. "Can you sip this? It'll warm your insides."

Clara didn't try to free her hands to take the cup, just parted her lips so Angela could lift the drink to her mouth.

With the women taking over Clara's care, Miles's hands itched to do something. He spoke quietly to Dinah. "How can I help?"

She shook her head as she eased Clara's bare feet into the pot of water. "Just stay close."

Clara gasped as her toes hit the liquid, and her mouth formed a thin line. Her eyes turned red as tears pooled in them.

He could stand it no longer. He reached out and brushed the loose hair back from her brow. "I'm so sorry." If only he could take this pain from her. He knew well how agonizing it could be to warm frozen limbs.

She turned those hurting eyes on him, drawing him closer. He moved his other hand to the blanket covering her, resting it on her arm.

Clara glanced at the seat beside him. "Can I move there?"

His chest squeezed and he looked to Dinah as he stood. She was already shifting the pot of water, so he scooped Clara from her chair.

Within seconds, he had her settled beside him. He wrapped both arms around her as she leaned into him, her head on his chest.

Air leaked out of her in a long audible exhale, and he tucked her closer, pressing a kiss to the blanket still covering her head. "You'll feel better soon."

Dinah sank back on her heels to study Clara, then her uncle, whom Naomi and Angela were assisting. Jericho and Jude sat on either side of the man, listening to his quiet murmurings. The rest of their group had gathered around.

Miles, Clara, and Dinah were probably the only people in the room who couldn't hear his words. Yet as much as he'd like to know exactly what happened—and why—he wouldn't pass up this chance to hold the woman who'd seeped into his heart so quickly, even before he realized it.

Jericho rose from his seat beside Hiram and came to kneel next to his wife, in front of Clara. He rested a hand on Dinah's shoulders. "Hiram seems fine, but exhausted. They're going to help him to bed. How's our patient here?"

Dinah gave him one of those gentle smiles she reserved for her husband. Once upon a time, Miles would have called the look sappy. But he had a better idea of the feelings behind it now. The intimacy of knowing this person knew and understood you so fully.

Miles stroked his thumb up and down Clara's arm, a gentle reminder to them both that he was here and wouldn't be leaving any time soon.

Dinah answered Jericho's question with, "She's better."

Jericho turned to Clara. "Your uncle said Holloway, Tillman, and Whitaker tied the two of you up before they all rode out. He said he doesn't know why, but that Holloway was having you do something with paperwork." His voice gentled more. "Do you feel up to telling what happened? We'll ride after them and see they're held accountable, but I'd like to know exactly what we're getting into."

Clara drew a shaky breath, her body tensing against him.

Miles tightened his hold, letting her know without words that she was safe now. That he wouldn't let anything else happen to her.

She glanced up at him, and he pushed the blanket back a little so he could see her face. Her eyes had turned glassy again, and a tear leaked down her cheek.

"Shh." He brushed it away with his thumb. "You're safe now." Maybe she did need words.

She shook her head, even more moisture welling in her eyes. "I'm so sorry."

Sorry? For what?

Something in her tone planted a rock in his gut.

She sniffed and returned her focus to Jericho.

Miles couldn't see her expression anymore, but he kept his thumb stroking her arm. Whatever she had to say, they'd face it together.

"Several days ago, Holloway asked me to...find something. He wanted me to look for the deed to your property. Here, in your house." Her voice trembled as she spoke. Actually, her entire body trembled.

He was focused so much on comforting her that it took a beat for her words to sink in.

The deed to...their house? To the ranch?

Why would Holloway want it? Had he discovered the sapphires?

He must have.

Had Clara done what he asked?

Of course not.

The man had tied her and her uncle and left them to freeze to death.

The vice clamping his chest eased enough for him to focus on what she was saying.

"He threatened my uncle. And the rest of you. Said if I didn't find the paper, he'd start causing *accidents*. That people would get hurt." Her gaze flicked to little Anna on the far side of the room, and he realized...

And then she tipped her chin up to Miles. "He named you especially."

CHAPTER 20

The guilt pooling in Clara's eyes had Miles's gut clenching. He wanted to tell her she didn't need to worry about him. But he couldn't interrupt her story. The fact that Holloway put her in this position made his blood heat.

She pressed her lips together, rolling them in as she looked back at Jericho. "I tried to put him off, but he gave me two days to find it. I told him there wasn't ever a time when the cabin was empty, so he said he would create a distraction. I didn't know what he would do. I thought…another campfire. Or gunshots. That's when Anna was taken." Her voice hitched. "I'm so sorry. I never meant for any of this to happen. I didn't know what to do. How to stop him."

Emotion burned Miles's eyes, clogging his throat.

How could he have not known Clara was suffering through this? Why hadn't she confided in him? He could have helped.

They all could have helped, if only she'd trusted them enough.

Trusted *him* enough.

Dinah rested a hand on Clara's arm through the blanket. "You were placed in an awful position. I'm so sorry."

His sister-in-law's gentleness seemed to increase Clara's tears, for several more leaked down her face. Her shoulders jerked in a sob. But then she caught herself and let out an audible breath. "Anyway, I found the deed in your trunk."

Jericho's face hardened. He looked…furious.

Clara shifted her gaze to Dinah, maybe seeing what Miles was seeing. But surely his oldest brother knew she hadn't betrayed them.

"I wasn't going to let him take it."

Dinah was nodding, her expression kind. "Of course you weren't."

"I thought maybe I could copy it and change some of the details so it was clear to a clerk that his was a forgery."

"That's smart." Dinah had taken on the role of encourager. He'd never appreciated her so much as in this moment.

"I thought it was going to work." The words squeaked out. "I sent the changed copy with the food yesterday. But then when Holloway showed up today and said we had to leave, he took me back to the camp and made me write another document." Her pitch was high, as if she fought emotion to get the story out. "It said you were signing over the property to our boss at the railroad. A man named Marcus Winston."

The name pricked at something in Miles's memory.

And from the gasp nearby, he wasn't the only one to recognize it.

"Winston?" Angela stepped closer, eyes wide and sparking. "Winston is part of this? He's the man I worked for. The one who turned dirty and assigned me to follow Jude to find this ranch. I thought…"

Jude stepped beside her, and she turned her focus to him. "I thought he'd been sentenced by the Treasury Department." Passion crept into her tone as she spoke. "It's just like him to wheedle out of the charges. You said…if he's Holloway's boss, then that means he works for the railroad now."

Clara nodded, her expression even more miserable, if that were possible. "Holloway said Winston was behind it all. The letter I wrote gives him ownership of the property on the Homestead deed. I changed the initials again, though, so as long as a clerk compares it to a log book, he'll realize something is amiss."

Jericho straightened, his expression hardening. "You staked our whole ranch on two little letters and the competence of a clerk?" He shot a look at Miles, and it wasn't hard to read his thoughts. *You trusted this woman. We could have lost everything.*

Confusion swirled inside him. Why hadn't Clara said something? She could have told him what was happening. He could have helped. Did she not trust him?

She twisted to look at Miles, fresh tears gathering. "I didn't know what else to do. He said he would hurt all of you if I didn't write the letter. And Uncle Hiram, and I couldn't let that happen. After what he did to Anna, I knew how far he'd go to get what he wants. I'm so sorry."

Her uncle. That blackguard threatened her uncle. And the rest of them, apparently. Clara must have been scared and torn between the two options. She did the best she could under the situation.

As he studied her watery gaze, he could see her heart. Her desperate desire to help—not hurt.

He cupped her face in his hands, using his thumbs to brush away the moisture on her cheeks. "You did the best you could in that position." He tucked her closer. "And it's all over. You're safe. I'm so glad you're safe."

Once more, a shuddering breath left her body, and she rested against him.

Jericho's tone didn't sound quite as forgiving, but not as angry as before. "Where's the real deed? Back in my trunk?"

Clara took in another deep inhale. "I didn't get a chance to put it back before Holloway came for us." She looked up at

Miles again. "I made an excuse to leave them on the way back to the camp and tucked it between the crates in the storage shed where we took shelter. It was the only place I knew of where it'd be safe, and you would certainly find it."

Miles met his older brother's gaze and raised his brows. Would Jericho see Clara had done the best she thought she could in the midst of a miserable situation? She'd protected them in every way she could think of.

Jericho's eyes softened a tiny bit more. He was acquiescing. Especially since they knew everything now.

Jericho's gaze turned distant as his mind clearly moved on to another thought. "Sounds like we're dealing with a different enemy than we realized." He glanced around at their other brothers and Eric, who'd come in from the barn. "I wonder if Holloway and his men are responsible for the rest of what's been happening around here? The butchered cow, the camp-fires, and the stranger who tried to get to the house."

Miles played back through the events in his mind. It seemed possible. Maybe not the stranger. Had he looked like one of the surveyors?

Clara shifted. "I don't know. I truly don't. I wouldn't have thought them that kind of people before he forced me to search for the deed. Now, I wouldn't put it past them."

Quiet settled over the group as they all worked through the question. Clara no longer trembled against him—a good sign. She needed sleep as much as her uncle. They all did.

Patsy approached from the cookstove, carrying a bowl. "You should eat. This soup will help warm you and bring back your strength."

Clara took the bowl from Patsy with a weak smile.

Jericho stood and shifted back to stand with the others. Ready to make plans.

Miles needed to be part of those plans. But he also needed to stay here with Clara. He couldn't imagine a time he'd be ready for her to leave his arms.

Thankfully, Jericho spoke loudly enough to include him. "We need to go after them at first light." He glanced around his brothers.

Jude spoke up. "I'm going. We have to get to the bottom of this, especially with Winston involved."

"Me too." Jonah gave a solid nod.

"I'd like to come." Clara's voice beside him caught him off guard.

Miles shifted to see her face.

"I'm not sure that's a good idea." Dinah spoke up, then turned to her husband. "She ought to stay here where it's safe. These men almost killed her once already."

But Clara's tone came stronger. "You might need me to confirm the documents are fake, assuming they're going straight to a land office."

That made sense, but he couldn't stomach the thought of her heading back out in the cold. Nor of her going near any of those men who'd just tried to kill her.

Clara turned back to Jericho. "I need to go with you."

Jericho studied her a heartbeat. Then he gave a slow nod. "It's up to you. We'll be there to protect you. It might not be an easy ride though."

"I'll be fine." Clara was a fighter. Gentle, completely giving of herself, and strong.

If she intended to ride with his brothers, there was nothing in the world that could keep him from going along too.

He gave Jericho a nod. "I'm going too."

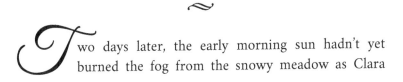

wo days later, the early morning sun hadn't yet burned the fog from the snowy meadow as Clara mounted her horse alongside Miles and Jericho, Jude, and Jonah. Puffs of steam rose from the horses' nostrils in the icy air. Her own breath clouded too.

Last night had been frigid, though they'd kept the campfire stoked and all slept close to it. They'd brought furs for cover, but it felt like she'd never be warm again.

No one spoke as they started out, Jericho in the lead. The surveyors' tracks weren't hard to follow in daylight, thanks to the snow still covering the landscape. Their direction hadn't been clear at first, but Jericho said they now seemed aimed toward Missoula Mills. And probably the land office there. The thought coiled in her gut.

Jericho pushed into a lope over the open land. Their quarry hadn't stuck to the main road, but traveled nearby. Maybe trying not to be seen by travelers, but the route left their tracks mostly undisturbed.

More than an hour later, the town buildings appeared through the trees ahead.

She glanced at Miles, who rode beside her. He sat tall in the saddle. Confident and determined. Those broad shoulders, the set of his jaw. He looked like a man who could protect her. Yet those warm eyes, they were gentle. Especially the way they looked at her now.

He nudged his horse closer to hers and spoke quietly. "How are you holding up?"

She gave a tight smile. "I'm all right. Just cold."

"Hopefully we can stay in Missoula Mills tonight. The hotel will be warm." That sounded like Heaven.

As they approached the outer edge of town, the surveyors' tracks merged onto the road, becoming impossible to decipher among all the other wagon and horse prints.

Jericho motioned for them to ride alongside him. "We should probably head straight for the land office. See if they've tried to register the bill of sale yet. But stay sharp. They could be anywhere in town. If they're watching, they might see us before we see them."

They didn't pass many people on their ride down the quiet street. Would the land office even be open yet? It must be about half past eight. Nine at the latest.

When they reached the squat clapboard building bearing a sign for the land office, Jericho swung from his saddle, and the rest of them followed suit.

They tied their horses to the rail in front of the door.

"Should we all come in?" Jude asked.

Jericho glanced back. "Probably a good idea. Strength in numbers." His gaze landed on Clara and softened. "They might need your word too, Miss Pendleton."

She nodded firmly. "I'll tell everything I know." She would do everything possible to make sure the Coulters didn't lose their ranch.

When they entered, the man sitting at a desk behind the counter stood and peered at them over his spectacles. He didn't speak, just waited with expectation.

Jericho stepped forward, his boots heavy on the wood floor. "Morning. I'm Jericho Coulter, and these are my brothers and a friend." He paused, maybe letting the clerk register their names. "We're wondering if a group of men, maybe four of them, stopped here in the last day to register a sale for our ranch."

The clerk's gaze narrowed on him. Was he thinking about the people who'd come here, or deciding how much to say?

As cold as she'd been two minutes ago, sweat dampened under her arms now. The thought that they might lose the ranch—or at least have to fight to prove ownership—was no small matter.

"There *were* some men." The clerk's gaze pinned on Jericho, his brow gathered. "You're Jericho Coulter? You do look familiar."

Jericho nodded down the line of them. "These are my brothers, Jonah, Jude, and Miles, and Miss Clara Pendleton." He turned back to the clerk. "You say they came in here?"

The clerk pursed his lips, and something in his expression settled. "Yesterday, late afternoon. Four of them, like you said. Tried to register a bill of sale for the Coulter ranch."

Tried to?

Her heart stuttered. They'd been here. But the clerk's words held a note of uncertainty.

The man shook his head. "The names on the documents didn't match up with what's in the ledger."

Relief washed through her, so strong it left her lightheaded.

Her changes had worked. She let out a slow breath. Maybe the first since she'd walked in this building.

Miles's hand slipped around hers, gripping tight.

Jericho leaned forward, his voice low and urgent. "What happened? Did they leave the documents with you?"

The clerk stood taller. "I refused to accept them. They weren't too happy about that, but there wasn't much they could do. Last I saw, they headed over to the hotel." He pointed out the window toward a large, two-story building down the street.

"Thank you, sir." Jericho reached out and shook the man's hand. "You may have just saved our ranch."

As they stepped back out onto the street, the cold wind biting their faces, Jude spoke up. "We headed to the hotel?"

"Yep." Jericho untied his horse while the rest of them did the same. "We can walk there."

Movement would help warm them.

Miles stayed at her side as they maneuvered the street, skirting frozen wheel ruts and animal droppings.

When they approached the hotel, two people stepped outside.

Another man jogged from the building across the street to enter where the first two had exited.

"Seems there's a lot of activity." Jonah murmured just loud enough for them all to hear.

Another group of people exited the building, this time a woman and man. The lady pulled her shawl tight around her, not nearly enough cover for the bitter cold.

Had something made them rush out without thinking through what they'd need?

The woman spoke loudly, going on about something, though they weren't close enough for her to make out the words. The couple turned the other direction. Maybe headed to the café she'd seen down the block.

A few minutes later, Jericho held the door open, and they stepped into the foyer of the hotel. This one wasn't nearly as big or fancy as the lodging in Fort Benton, but at least the place was warm.

At the moment, it seemed rather crowded too. The clerk behind the desk looked harried, his face pale as he spoke to a group of men gathered across from him.

It was impossible not to hear the conversation.

"I found him just like that." The clerk's voice trembled. "Lying there in his room, a knife in his belly."

She exchanged a glance with Miles. A murder in the hotel?

"What's his name?" The fellow who asked looked like he might have been the man running toward the hotel a few minutes ago. He asked the question with authority and was writing in a book as he spoke.

"He registered as Marcus Winston. Been here three days."

CHAPTER 21

*T*he name struck Miles like a physical blow. Marcus Winston? The man who had hired the surveyors to steal their land. *And* ordered that Clara and her uncle be murdered.

He'd also tried to kill Jude and Angela a couple years ago.

Now, he was dead?

Clara gripped his elbow, her face even paler than before. He slipped his arm around her waist. Maybe this wasn't proper in public, but she probably needed this contact as much as he did.

"Was anyone here with him? Did he have visitors?"

Miles couldn't see the face of the man asking questions to check if he wore a badge. Missoula Mills didn't have law—or at least they hadn't before now—but maybe this was a new sheriff come to town. The place had certainly grown large enough to need someone to keep the peace.

"Not that I know of." The clerk frowned. "I don't keep tabs on comings and goings unless someone stops to ask a question. There were a few fellows who came through yesterday who weren't registered as guests. But they seemed to know right where they were going."

They had to be the surveyors.

Jericho stepped closer to the desk, drawing the attention of the strangers. "Sorry to barge in, but I couldn't help hearing. You said Marcus Winston was killed here?"

The man who'd been asking questions swiveled to face Jericho fully. "Do you know him?"

"Not personally, but we've come looking for him. Him and four other men who work for him."

The man's eyes narrowed on Jericho. "I'm Deputy John Hanson. New to the position here in Missoula Mills. What's your business with Winston?"

Jericho lowered his voice. "It's a long story, but the short of it is that Winston hired four surveyors to steal the deed to our family's ranch. They forged a bill of sale and tried to file it at the land office yesterday."

Harris's eyebrows shot up. "That's quite an accusation. And you are?"

"Jericho Coulter. These are my brothers Jonah, Jude, and Miles. And Miss Clara Pendleton, a friend of ours."

Deputy Hanson's eyes widened slightly. "Coulter, you said? Of the Coulter Ranch?"

"That's right." Jericho's voice stayed grim, but Miles wouldn't have expected a new deputy to have heard about their ranch. They tried to keep a low profile.

The deputy flipped back a page in his notebook. "And you said there were four other men with him? Can you tell me about them?"

Jericho looked to Clara, and she spoke up to give descriptions of the surveyors. Miles briefly explained what they'd done to her and her uncle. And relief, for talking about it was still hard. As he finished, he seemed to sense her struggle. He tightened his arm around her.

She and her uncle had almost died. And now another man, Winston, really was dead. What evil his greed had caused. Was

Winston the one behind the entire scheme, or had he been organizing it for someone else?

And was Holloway the one who killed him? A shiver slipped through her. Had the men she and her uncle traveled with for weeks murdered a man in cold blood?

Deputy Hanson finished writing and looked back up at them. "If Winston hired those men to steal from you, and now he's dead..." He let the implication hang in the air.

The clerk spoke through the heavy silence. "Those sound like some of the men who came through here last evening."

Miles's eyes snapped to the clerk. "You saw them? The surveyors?"

The clerk nodded, his face pale. "They came in, maybe an hour or so before I found Mr. Winston. Headed straight up the stairs like they knew where they were going."

Deputy Hanson stepped closer, his voice low and urgent. "Did you see them leave?"

"I...I can't be sure." The clerk looked apologetic. "It was busy in here. Lots of folks coming and going. I wasn't watching."

The deputy turned back to Miles. "I'm inclined to believe your story, Mr. Coulter. And if these men did murder Winston, they need to be brought to justice."

Miles nodded. "Agreed. We can't let them get away with this, or with trying to steal our land."

"Do you have any idea where they might have gone? If they left town?" the deputy asked.

Jericho straightened. "They came from our ranch, which is northeast of town. I suspect they'll be going west, as far from here as they can get."

Deputy Hanson nodded. "All right. Let me get a couple men together, and we'll ride out with you. We need to find these fellows before they get too far."

"I'll come too," Jonah spoke up.

Jericho glanced at his brother and nodded. He turned to Jude

Miles fought the urge to elbow him as Jude handed Clara her bag and bedroll.

"Thank you." She took her belongings with the grace she always displayed.

Ah well.

There would be other chances to kiss this woman, he would make sure of it. A lifetime of chances, if she agreed to what he planned to ask. Soon.

CHAPTER 22

lara walked between Jude and Miles the next morning down the quiet street. Though no wind whipped around her like on the mountain, the cold's icy fingers found every exposed piece of skin. They would be at the café soon though.

Beside her, Miles jerked to a stop.

She turned to him, as did Jude.

He faced another man who must have stepped from the alleyway beside them. He looked familiar. Gil? Not Gil, but the fellow looked remarkably like him.

"Sampson?" Jude breathed the name as he stepped closer. "Where did you come from? What are you doing here?"

Clara hung back. That must be Miles's other brother. The one who'd left the ranch a few months ago to work at a different mine. Grief had weighed Miles's voice when he told her about him. Sampson was the next brother up in age, the one Miles had always been closest to.

Jude gripped Sampson's shoulders and pulled him into a quick hug.

But Sampson barely returned it, looking stiff in the hold. He pulled back after a short moment.

He glanced between his two brothers, then his gaze snagged on Clara before moving back to Miles and Jude. "You need to get out of town. Now. Go back to the ranch and stay there."

"Come with us." Miles stepped toward him. His voice sounded almost…defensive. Or maybe determined.

"I can't. Not yet." His gaze darted to the street, then back to his brothers. "You need to leave. Do you understand?"

Miles took a tiny step closer. "Are you in trouble? There's a lawman here now. We'll all help."

Sampson stepped back, shaking his head. "Don't. You don't know what you're messing with. Get out of town. Go back to the ranch. And don't leave again."

With one more backward step, Sampson turned and disappeared down the alley as quickly as he had come.

Miles started after him, but Jude caught his arm. "Let him go."

Miles spun to him. "He needs to come with us."

Jude shook his head, his brow creasing. "Jericho and I've talked about it. I don't know what Sampson is mixed up in, but he's old enough to make his own choices. All we can do is be there when he's ready to come home."

The pain in Miles's expression made her step closer. She knew well the grief of losing someone she loved.

As the fight drained from Miles's shoulders, he turned toward the cafe again.

She slipped under his arm, wrapping an arm around his waist. Maybe she shouldn't show so much affection in public—though the streets were deserted, so only Jude was likely to see this touch.

This situation was far from normal.

The pain of knowing what Holloway and his cronies had

done, to her, to her uncle, and to the Coulters in attempting to steal the ranch.

The shock at realizing they'd probably gone so far as to kill Winston.

The worry of what might be happening with Jericho and Jonah as they went after the scoundrels.

And now the grief at seeing his lost brother and hearing such a dire warning.

Then watching that brother choose to walk away—again.

Nothing about this situation was normal. And if her arm around his waist could help bring Miles solace, she wouldn't hesitate.

Miles placed his hand around her side, and they continued on to the café in heavy silence.

Her mind wouldn't stop spinning with questions about Sampson's cryptic warning.

What kind of trouble could he be in? And why did he want them to leave town so urgently?

In the quiet restaurant, only a man and woman sat at a table near a window. The couple seemed deep in quiet conversation, not even looking up when they entered.

Jude led them to a table on the opposite side of the room but still adjacent to the row of windows facing the street.

The gray-haired woman who'd served them night before hurried out with a kettle and three tin mugs. "Coffee?"

Clara nodded, murmuring her thanks as the woman poured the steaming liquid. She wrapped her chilled fingers around the mug, letting the warmth seep into her skin.

Miles and Jude accepted their drinks as well, but the heaviness in the air remained thick.

As she lifted the mug to her lips, movement outside the window caught her eye. She paused and focused on the two figures across the street.

iles." She nodded toward the window. "Isn't that ...npson?"

His head snapped up, his eyes narrowing as he took in the scene.

Jude leaned forward, his brow furrowing. "Who's that with him?"

Sampson spoke to a shorter, unfamiliar man. The stranger's face was obscured by a wide-brimmed hat, but something about his posture sent a shiver down her spine. Yet, he didn't prick her memory at all.

Miles leaned forward, squinting. "You don't think it could be Jedidiah, do you? Didn't Gil say he was short and thin, like an old miner?"

The man certainly fit that description. She glanced between Miles and Jude. She'd not heard them speak of a man by that name.

The brothers held a gaze for a moment, then Miles turned back to her. "You remember I told you about Mick, Jess's father who stole from us?"

She nodded. He'd not given a lot of detail, but she'd gotten the feeling the man was a significant threat they still protected against.

"Jedidiah is his right-hand man. From what Gil says, he looks harmless but is the cruelest criminal he's ever met. He had his guards beat Gil unconscious."

Her middle twisted as she turned back for another look at the short, slight villain.

He was gone. Sampson too.

"Where did they go?" She leaned forward to see more of the street.

"Did they duck inside the saloon?" Jude nodded to the building the men had stood in front of.

Miles blew out a breath. "Should we go look for them?"

Jude didn't answer right away, just studied the structure

She squinted against the bright morning sunlight reflecting off the dirty snow.

As her eyes adjusted, two familiar figures exited a building down the street. Was that the deputy's office?

Hope flared in her chest.

Miles saw them too. He strode forward, calling out. "Jericho! Jonah!"

The men turned, then moved toward them, meeting them in the middle of the street.

"We got them." Jericho spoke without preamble. "All four surveyors. The deputy has them locked up until a judge comes through."

Relief crashed through her like a wave.

It was over. The threat to the Coulters' ranch was gone. Holloway and the others would be punished. And Winston had already received more than his due.

Before she could linger on the sadness of the way he'd ended, Jericho held up some papers. "And these are the forged documents."

Her middle plummeted. She'd hoped to never see them again. Yet not only was she faced with them now, Jericho and Jonah had no doubt examined them thoroughly.

They must hate her.

But when Jericho faced her, his expression softened. "I'm more grateful than I can say for your quick thinking. You were in a terrible position, but your changes on these documents are what stopped those scoundrels from succeeding."

A twinkle slipped into the older man's gaze. "The deputy said he doesn't need these for evidence, so we're free to do what we want with them." He extended them toward her.

Did she have to take them, these papers that proved what a fool she was? She had no desire to store them away as a memento of her mistakes. But, unsure what else to do, she accepted them from his outstretched hand.

He reached into his coat pocket and pulled out a tinderbox. As he struck the flint to steel, she sent a sideways look at Miles to see if he had any idea what was happening. In the middle of the main street, no less.

Miles shrugged, so she turned back to watch Jericho.

His first spark caught in the wool, and he blew until a small flame lit. Then he took the papers from her with a wink, and placed a corner of the sheets in the fire.

The paper's edge darkened, and orange flame followed the burnt line up the page.

She could only watch as fire devoured the forgeries. Burning her neat script—and along with it, the lies, the deception, the guilt.

With each passing second, with each flick of the flames, she felt lighter. Freer.

The fire threatening his fingers, Jericho crouched on the ground, releasing the documents onto the frozen mud.

When nothing remained but a small pile of embers, he stood and met her gaze, understanding and compassion shining in his eyes. "It's over now. You did good, Clara."

Emotion clogged her throat, burning her eyes. She could only nod.

Miles slipped an arm around her waist, pulling her to his side. She leaned into him, relishing his solid strength and warmth.

He pressed a kiss to her temple. "See? I told you it would all work out."

Somehow, it had.

She looked into the face she loved so much. "You were right."

~

*T*he sun glinted off the river as Miles walked beside Clara that afternoon, their hands entwined. A sense of peace wrapped around him, so different from the tension of the past days. Jericho and Jonah had gone to look for Sampson and finish a bit of business in town, and they would all start back to the ranch in the morning.

The gold tints in her brown hair shimmered in the light. Now was the time. He had to tell her how he felt.

He cleared his throat. "Clara, I've been talking with Jericho, and we were thinking...we could use another man to help out on the ranch. Especially with the possible trouble from Mick McPharland." He paused. "Jericho plans to ask your uncle if he'd like to stay on and work with us."

She stopped, a slow smile spreading across her face. "I can't speak for Uncle Hiram, but I think he'll say yes." Her green eyes sparkled. "I hope he'll say yes."

His heart swelled. This was the opening he needed. "That's good. Good." He took a deep breath, facing her fully. "I've come to love everything about you. Your strength, your compassion, your spirit." He reached for her other hand, holding both of hers in his. "I would be honored if you'd consider staying on too. And allow me to court you."

Tears welled in her eyes, but her smile only grew. The tendons at her throat worked. "I'd like that more than anything."

His heart picked up speed as he met her gaze. The love shining back at him made his chest ache.

How had he ever been happy without this woman? He lifted his hands to cradle her face, his thumbs brushing away the moisture on her cheeks.

He lowered his head, a little at a time, giving her space to pull away if she wanted. But she tilted her chin up, meeting him halfway.

Their lips brushed, soft and tentative. A caress of skin against skin, a whisper of breath. Then Clara sighed, her body melting into his, and he deepened the kiss.

Miles wrapped his arms around her, pulling her close. She fit so perfectly, like she was made to be here. With him.

Her fingers slid into his hair, sending sparks down his spine.

Far too soon, he forced himself to slow down. To ease back. Lord willing, there would be many kisses ahead of them. He wouldn't rush her.

But he rested his forehead against hers, unwilling to let even an inch of space come between them. "You're the best thing that ever happened to me, Clara Pendleton. I don't know how I ever thought I could let you go."

A smile curved her mouth, and she played with the hair at the nape of his neck. "God brought us back together, and that's all that matters."

Indeed.

He settled his arms tighter around her waist, reveling in the feel of her, the rightness of it. *Thank You, Lord.*

No matter what challenges lay ahead, they would face them together...with the One who loved them most of all.

I pray you loved Miles and Clara's story!

Sampson finally gets his story in the final book in the series! What a surprise he's in for as the danger to his family's ranch comes to an impossible climax!

- Marriage of convenience
- Surprise ward
- Ready-made family

- Bad boy/black sheep
- Wounded hero/caretaker heroine
- Forced proximity

Turn the page for a sneak peek of *Saving the Mountain Man's Legacy,* the next book in the Brothers of Sapphire Ranch series!

SNEAK PEEK: SAVING THE MOUNTAIN MAN'S LEGACY

CHAPTER ONE

OCTOBER, 1870
WILDERNESS NEAR CANVAS CREEK, MONTANA TERRITORY

Almost to the mine.

As Sampson Coulter's horse neared the last curve in the trail, he straightened in his saddle, stretching out his back. After working so many months in McPharland's tunnels, his body had forgotten how it felt to spend hours in the saddle. He should have left Missoula Mills earlier yesterday. Then he wouldn't have had to stop for the night in that old trapper's cabin. At least he'd had shelter before the rest of the long ride today.

Now he barely had time to check in with Mick, hitch the horses quickly, and get back to Jedidiah with the wagon load he'd been sent to retrieve. He didn't relish sleeping in the cold again, especially with the blasting powder packed carefully in the wagon bed, but he'd have to if he didn't want to drive through the night. That stuff became unreliable in icy temperatures.

As the trees opened up around him, he raised a hand to shield his eyes from the bright light reflecting off the snow around the mountain that hid McPharland's mine. Even though the sun shone high overhead, the cold wind bit through his coat and sent chills up his spine. It wouldn't be long now until the snow started falling.

A strange noise sounded, but not from the direction of the mountain. A shrill cry to the right of it. Not a fox or any kind of wildcat.

Was that…a baby?

Another cry confirmed the sound. What on earth?

His mind whirled with possibilities, and he turned his horse that direction. He approached the source of the noise, and as he slowed his mount, a small wagon came into view, partially hidden by a cluster of pine trees. A young woman stood beside it, her back turned to him as she bent over something in the wagon bed.

The baby's cries grew louder, and the woman's voice rose in

frustration. "Shh, shh, little one. I know, I know. Just give me a moment."

Sampson pulled his horse to a halt a few feet away and dismounted. "Ma'am? Is everything all right?"

The woman spun around, her eyes wide.

As he took her in, the force of her appearance—such a small dainty thing out here in this wilderness tainted so fully by McPharland's presence—caught him off guard. He braced his feet to keep from backing a step.

She stared back, mirroring his shock. Then the babe wailed. Her attention snapped to the child on the wagon in front of her. The squirming bundle, who had been stripped bare, kicked legs. The infant must be half frozen in this wind.

The woman wrestled to cover the babe with a strip of unwieldy cloth. "I just...it won't... Be still, Ruby. We have to get you..."

She seemed to be having a rough time of it, with one hand firm on a little leg and the other trying to wrap the fabric around the child.

He stepped closer, moving up to her side but keeping enough space between them she hopefully wouldn't think him a threat. "How can I help?" He'd never put on a diaper before, but he could offer an extra set of hands.

She spared the quickest of glances his way, but a fresh wail from the child made her cringe. She spoke louder to be heard over the cries. "Can you hold her feet? Gently. She keeps squirming, and I don't want to get the clean diaper soiled."

He reached in to grip the tiny ankles in one hand. How had he never realized how massive his hands were? But the moment his calloused fingers closed around those toothpick ankles, he brought in the second hand. He couldn't grip them tight. This babe was barely bigger than his hand, and the ankles weren't much larger around than his thumb. Any little squeeze might snap the bones in two.

The woman worked around his gangly arms, wrapping the cloth in a neat hold that hadn't seemed possible when she was fighting with the material seconds ago. As she pulled the knot tight, she murmured, "Keep hold of her another minute while I get the rest of it off."

He checked the pressure in his hands once more as the woman worked the babe's tiny hands out of her sleeves. Did she intend to strip the child fully? It was too cold out here for all that. This infant couldn't be more than a few days old. How could she even survive this tiny?

But when she turned the babe's shoulders to release the back of the gown underneath her, a wave of stench wafted up. Ugh.

He pressed his mouth closed and tried not to breathe through his nose as he turned away. That diaper must not have done its job well at all.

He had to look away to get a clear breath, and that was the moment she said, "You can let go now. Thank you."

Whew. Thank goodness. He obeyed, releasing the babe's ankles and stepping back. Once more, he turned his head for a clean breath, but that gust of smell must have singed his nose hairs. He couldn't get shed of the odor.

"That's my girl. All better." The woman murmured quiet words now as she lifted the babe up to her shoulder, tucking the blanket around her.

He could no longer see the infant, but her cries turned to shuddering whimpers. The sound twisted something inside him. Such a fragile, helpless little thing.

The woman swayed and bounced as she held child, whispering something he couldn't hear. Then she lifted her eyes to him, a hint of embarrassment tinging them. "Thank you for your help."

He nodded, then shuffled back a step and glanced around. "Your man gone somewhere?" He'd not thought of that before.

Why were these two here alone? And so close to Mick's mine? Surely her husband didn't work for the man.

Mick didn't take on families. Only single men who could live in the bunk room and work in the caves.

She lifted her chin, but it did little to raise her stature. She must be a head and a half shorter than him. Not even five foot if he had to guess. "I'm looking for my father. He works in a mine near here."

His body tensed, but he kept his face casual. "What's his name?" A mine near here had to mean Mick's operation. Was her father Cornwall, the new fellow who came a fortnight ago? He didn't see old enough to have a grown daughter, though this woman didn't look much older than a girl herself.

She was scrutinizing him. Wondering what kind of men who father worked with? "Jedidiah Hampton."

He blinked, the reaction slipping out before he could stop it. Jedidiah...Hampton? Surely she didn't mean the tyrant who McPharland depended on to accomplish all his dirty work. Had he ever heard Jedidiah's surname? He couldn't summon a single name that he'd heard put with that first name.

Just *Jedidiah*, like the first man had only been named Adam. Except Adam had been breathed to life by the Almighty, and Jedidiah had probably been created directly by Satan himself. The man delighted in evil more than any person Sampson had ever met.

The woman studied him, so he tried to clear any remnants of shock from his expression and raised his brows. "What does he look like exactly?"

She frowned and gave a half-shrug. "I don't know. Taller than me but..." She glanced above Sampson's eyes. "Not near as tall as you. Hair darker than mine but with gray mixed in."

That wasn't a very detailed description. It described Jedidiah though. How many men by that name could there be in this area? But... "You say you're his daughter?"

Jedidiah always seemed more demon than human. How could he possibly have a child? Or rather...how could he have sired a young woman as pretty as this one?

But if she truly was her father's daughter, she would be wily. Devious. Innocent in appearance but capable of great evil. He'd best be on guard.

And he should also make certain they were speaking of the same man.

Once more, he worked for a casual tone. "I know a man named Jedidiah, but I don't know his surname. Do you know whose mine your father works in?"

McPharland possessed the only mine in this area, as far as she knew, but this woman might have gotten off track in her search.

She squinted. "A man named Mick?" It came out as a question, as though she needed him to confirm.

His middle churned. Her words confirmed all he needed.

He let his eyes roam her face. She did have the same small, condensed features as Jedidiah. On her, they looked delicate and lovely, though on her father, they only made him blend in with a crowd. Like an old miner who's outlived his prime.

Her eyes were different than her father's though, wide and clear blue. Jedidiah's were dark and narrowed. Or maybe that was simply from the constant glare he gave everyone he deigned to speak to.

The babe on her shoulder began to fuss again, and the woman resumed swaying. "Can you tell me where I can find my father?"

Sampson sent a glance toward the mountain. No one had come out, and they were mostly hidden from view, but that didn't mean a guard wasn't watching. If this truly was Jedidiah's daughter, the man might be using her to prove Sampson's loyalty. He'd need to do as she asked, as much as he thought Jedidiah would want anyway. Certainly he couldn't allow her to interfere with his orders, but letting her ride along behind him wouldn't slow him down.

He leveled his gaze on her. "I actually just left your father in Missoula Mills. He sent me back for supplies. It will take me about a half hour to hitch the team and load up, then you can follow me back to him if you'd like. It's a full day's ride, and since we're starting midday, we'll need to stay the night on the road. There's a little trapper's cabin I usually bed down in. It's a bit drafty, but we can start a fire and keep warm."

As he spoke, the reality of what he was suggesting settled in. She had a newborn baby. It couldn't be healthy for the child to spend so many hours in the cold, then sleep in a shack that barely kept out the wind. And the woman… How long since she'd given birth? Could she even drive a team?

And the biggest question of all…where was her husband?

He tipped his head. "Is your husband close by? I can wait a little while, or else give you directions to the main road."

Once more, that pert chin tipped up. "I'm not married. But if you'll give me those directions, I won't hold you up any longer."

Not married.

The words sunk like a weight around his shoulders. He couldn't let her go alone. Especially not with that tiny bundle in her arms.

He needed to get her to Jedidiah. And he had to get the powder there quickly.

He glanced at her wagon. She didn't have much loaded in it. A few crates and a rocking chair. He could probably fit them in the wagon with the blasting powder. Except the rocking chair. He couldn't lay anything heavy on the powder, so that would have to stay.

"I'll tell you what— Let me get my team and wagon ready, then we'll move your things into mine, and I can drive the both of you. That way you can have both hands free to take care of

Little Bit there." He nodded to the babe, who'd begun to make little mewling noises.

The woman frowned. "I'd rather take my wagon. If you'll just tell me how to get there, I'll be on my way."

He fought to hold in his sigh. "I can tell you, ma'am, but Jedidiah would not look on me kindly for sending his daughter and grandbaby off into the wilderness on their own. 'Specially when headed the same way with a wagon that has plenty of room for 'em."

She added a pinched mouth to her frown. "I don't want to be a bother."

Was there a polite way to say how much more frustrating she was being keeping him standing here when he had a schedule to keep? His brother Gil could have managed it, but Sampson would do best not to try it. He did offer a smile. "I'd appreciate you letting me help, ma'am. Your father being Jedidiah and all."

That list bit seemed to bring her around, for she finally sighed. "All right then. Should I follow you with my team?"

He shook his head. "Stay here and get your things packed up. I'll be back soon."

He'd best make up all the time he could, for surely traveling with a woman and babe would slow him down. And he didn't relish Jedidiah's reaction if he kept the man waiting.

Chapter Two

Jewel Hampton's heart pounded against her ribs. Was it really a good idea to travel with a man she'd just met? Leave her own wagon and team behind, putting her and Ruby at his mercy?

If he was as trustworthy as he seemed, she would be much better off not having to worry about handling the team. And he was Father's employee.

He didn't return right away, so she used the time to dress Ruby. "I'm sorry I kept you in the blanket so long, sweet one." She pulled on the babe's long-sleeved undergarment and then her flannel gown before swaddling her again in the blanket—this time far more securely than before.

All their belongings were still packed, so she should be ready to move everything over as soon as he brought his wagon.

Her only other choice would be to follow his wagon with her own rig. Driving and caring for Ruby as best she could. That meant Ruby would have to lay in her basket most of the time. Then they'd have to stop the wagon to feed the babe. Then the trip would take longer than the day he'd said.

And now that the weather had turned cold, she needed to find her father as quickly as possible, get enough money to live on for a little while, then find a safe place for them to settle.

She worked to still her whirling thoughts. Whatever it took to reach her father, she had to do it quickly. Even if that included riding in this stranger's wagon for a day.

Besides, she wasn't completely defenseless. In addition to the revolver she had tucked in the hidden pocket of her skirt, she also had the rifle. She wouldn't hesitate to pull either weapon if she needed to protect herself and Ruby.

The crunching of wagon wheels across the ground sounded behind her, and she turned to see two horses pulling a wagon into view. One of the animals had the same coloring as one of the horses that often pulled Oren's wagon—brown with black main and tail.

The man drove the team, and halted them with his wagon alongside hers. He didn't stop to talk, just set the brake and jumped to the ground, then started hauling the boxes and barrels from her rig and positioning them in the bed of his own. She'd debated over what to bring, but had ended up packing most of their clothes and blankets and food, as well as a few books. She'd not known whether she should bring furniture or not. It seemed like each house would have its own, so hauling hers with her would be a waste. But then, she'd never purchased a new house, nor rented a room, so she hadn't been sure. Mama's rocker was the one piece that felt like it belonged more to *her* than to their house.

She settled Ruby in her basket, then untied the goat from behind her wagon. "Come on, Camelot. The grass is just as good over here." The nanny had begun eating the moment they stopped, and complained with a *maa* as Jewel tugged her away from the underbrush so she could tie the rope to the new wagon.

As she worked, she kept an eye on the man. He moved efficiently, no sign of strain as he hefted her belongings into his wagon. Belongings that had taken every bit of her strength to push up into the bed. It was hard to gauge his character from his actions, but he seemed focused and purposeful. Efficient, not sparing a glance her way as he arranged the items to fit.

Everything fit neatly, just as he'd said, with his cargo taking up only a portion of the wagon bed. He'd tucked her belongings around the outer edges. When he reached for her mother's rocking chair, the last item remaining, he paused.

Then he settled it back in her wagon. "We'll need to leave the chair here with your rig." He spoke casually, already moving to climb onto her rig to reposition it for storage.

"No." The word flew out before she could temper it. She inhaled a breath to steady herself. "I can't leave the chair behind. Just put it on top of the boxes."

He shook his head. "Nothing can on top of these crates. They're too fragile."

Frustration welled in her chest. Why was he being so difficult about this? "You need to figure something else out then, because I'm not leaving my mother's rocking chair. I need it for the baby."

The man frowned, his brow furrowing. "You can get it when you come back this way."

"I'm not planning to come back here." Jewel fought to keep her voice steady, though it trembled with emotion. "That rocking chair is one of the few things of my mother's I have left. I'd sooner drive my own wagon than leave it behind."

For a long moment, he simply stared at her, his expression unreadable. Then, with a sigh, he moved to her wagon and hefted the rocking chair into his arms. He carried it to his own wagon and tied it to the back of the wagon's bench, positioned above the bed so it rested on none of the crates.

Relief flooded through Jewel. Perhaps he wasn't as heartless as he seemed. When he finished, he drove her team away, saying he'd park the wagon and pasture the horses somewhere nearby.

Ruby had started her hungry cry, the sign she wouldn't be held off from food much longer.

"All right then." Jewel picked up the wicker basket by its two woven handles, making faces at the babe as she carried her to the front of the man's wagon. "I have a feeding bottle ready for you. I know you're hungry."

Ruby's cries eased into a shuddering sob as she studied Jewel's face, those wide blue eyes so desperate. "You're so pitiful when you're hungry."

She placed the basket on the bench and hauled herself up, then positioned it between her and where the man would sit. The babe would be a nice buffer.

By the time the man returned, she had the babe cradled in her arms, the feeding bottle's rubber nipple between her rosebud lips. Ruby drank hungrily, her eyes closed and jaw working as she suckled.

The man didn't speak, just strode around to his side of the wagon and stepped up into his seat. He gave Ruby a sideways look as he settled, taking up the reins. Then he focused ahead, released the brake, and shook the reins. "Walk on."

The wagon lurched into motion, and she braced her feet against the buckboard, gripping Ruby tightly as they started off.

As the wagon rolled along the rutted ground, she sneaked glances at the man beside her. He kept his gaze fixed forward, his hands steady. The silence stretched between them, broken only by the creaking of the wagon, the click of the horses' hooves on rocks, and the occasional snuffle from Ruby as she drank.

Finally, Jewel cleared her throat. "I don't believe I caught your name."

"Sampson. Sampson Coulter, ma'am." He looked at her briefly before returning his attention to the road.

"Well, Mr. Coulter, I appreciate you giving us a ride." She shifted Ruby in her arms to reposition the bottle.

"No trouble." His tone was polite but distant. "And you are...?"

"Jewel Hampton."

He shot her a look, brows lowered. "Hampton is your... married name?"

A question she should have expected, and he must have realized exactly what he was asking, for he jerked his focus back to the horses. "Never mind. It's nice to meet you, Mrs. Hampton."

With Hampton being her father's name, he was no doubt thinking she must have lied about something.

Best she set him straight. And consider changing her name if she planned to raise Ruby as her own. Or...maybe that wouldn't be necessary, for soon she wouldn't be around people who knew her father.

She sat a little straighter. "*Miss* Hampton. I'm not married. Ruby isn't my daughter by birth, but was given to me to raise."

She motioned to the feeding bottle. "Thus the reason we travel with a goat and this feeder."

Mr. Coulter eyed her once more, then his gaze dipped down to Ruby. "Someone gave you their child? Forever?"

Something in his tone made a small tug at her cheeks, though the situation no humor. "I...well, yes. I think so."

His focus rose back up to her face, his brows lifting. "You think so?"

Heat flared through her, and she fought to keep from stammering again. "Yes. I mean...yes." Now she couldn't keep her flush down. She huffed out a breath. "She was left on my doorstep. I came outside one afternoon and there lay this basket, with Ruby inside, and a box of blankets and diapers. Even this bottle and the goat."

She sent him a glare. "So yes, I'm assuming they meant for me to raise her as my own. No one's been back for her, so she and I are carrying on like this will be forever."

She glanced down at the cherubic face that had immediately latched hold of her heart. After two weeks and everything they'd been through together, she couldn't imagine having to turn the babe back over to someone else. And if the someone was who she thought it was, she didn't anticipate being asked to give Ruby back.

Mr. Coulter still stared at her, and now his jaw had dropped open a little, just enough to reveal the shadows of his lower teeth.

She fought a giggle. This big strapping man had been thoroughly stunned speechless. Well, that made two of them.

At last, he found his voice. "Someone just abandoned their child with you? And you never found out who?"

She shrugged, looking down at Ruby's peaceful face. "I have my suspicions. But I never saw them again."

"Did you not try to find them? Make them take responsibility?" His voice rose with indignation.

"I understood why they did it." Jewel kept her tone soft, though her heart clenched. "They needed help. And I'm glad to give it. Ruby will have the best care I can provide." And all the love she could ever want.

He shook his head, turning back to the road. "Ain't right, leaving a babe like that. Anything could've happened to her."

"But it didn't. And she has me now." Jewel lifted her chin.

Mr. Coulter turned quiet again, but not very long this time. "So that's why you're looking for your father."

Something in his tone made her bristle. "I need to move closer to town. Where I can have...access to things. I only wanted to let him know I'd be leaving." That wasn't quite true. She needed money, something she and Mama had never had to worry over. But they'd also never needed to leave the little house in the valley.

He snorted, a sound that unsettled something in her middle.

She waited for him to explain, but he remained quiet. Should she ask what that meant? Maybe she didn't want to know.

And really, did she need his opinion? He knew nothing of her and her life. Nor did he need to.

She settled back on the bench and tipped the bottle higher so Ruby could get the last of the milk. All she had to do now was care for her sweet daughter and count the hours until she reached the next step in their new life.

Get SAVING THE MOUNTAIN MAN'S LEGACY, the FINAL book in the Brothers of Sapphire Ranch series, at your favorite retailer!

Did you enjoy Miles and Clara's story? I hope so!
Would you take a quick minute to leave a review where you purchased the book?
It doesn't have to be long. Just a sentence or two telling what you liked about the story!

To receive a free book and get updates when new Misty M. Beller books release, go to https://mistymbeller.com/freebook

ALSO BY MISTY M. BELLER

Brothers of Sapphire Ranch

Healing the Mountain Man's Heart

Marrying the Mountain Man's Best Friend

Protecting the Mountain Man's Treasure

Earning the Mountain Man's Trust

Winning the Mountain Man's Love

Pretending to be the Mountain Man's Wife

Guarding the Mountain Man's Secret

Saving the Mountain Man's Legacy

Sisters of the Rockies

Rocky Mountain Rendezvous

Rocky Mountain Promise

Rocky Mountain Journey

The Mountain Series

The Lady and the Mountain Man

The Lady and the Mountain Doctor

The Lady and the Mountain Fire

The Lady and the Mountain Promise

The Lady and the Mountain Call

This Treacherous Journey

This Wilderness Journey

This Freedom Journey (novella)

This Courageous Journey

This Homeward Journey

This Daring Journey

This Healing Journey

Call of the Rockies

Freedom in the Mountain Wind

Hope in the Mountain River

Light in the Mountain Sky

Courage in the Mountain Wilderness

Faith in the Mountain Valley

Honor in the Mountain Refuge

Peace in the Mountain Haven

Grace on the Mountain Trail

Calm in the Mountain Storm

Joy on the Mountain Peak

Brides of Laurent

A Warrior's Heart

A Healer's Promise

A Daughter's Courage

Hearts of Montana

Hope's Highest Mountain

Love's Mountain Quest

Faith's Mountain Home

Honor's Mountain Promise

Texas Rancher Trilogy

The Rancher Takes a Cook

The Ranger Takes a Bride

The Rancher Takes a Cowgirl

Wyoming Mountain Tales

A Pony Express Romance

A Rocky Mountain Romance

A Sweetwater River Romance

A Mountain Christmas Romance

www.ingramcontent.com/pod-product-compliance
Lightning Source LLC
Jackson TN
JSHW081427040125
76500JS00004B/71